AF271709

Metamorphosis

Book 1

The Rebirth

Adam Kruszynski

ISBN: 978-1-7772766-0-7 Print

ISBN: 978-1-7772766-1-4 Ebook

www.metamorphosisbookseries.com

Dedicated to my wife Natasha, a lover of reading

Contents

Chapter 1: Friday Debate

Anne and Genne Manning rushed through the side door of prestigious Memorial Hall at Harvard University. This eighteenth century structure was modeled after a building at the University of Oxford. More specifically, the Sanders Theatre they were entering was inspired by Oxford's Sheldonian Theatre. Sanders is renowned for its acoustics and a rich history of speakers including Winston Churchill, Martin Luther King Jr., and Mikhail Gorbachev. Today however, it was not filled with scholars or politicians but a diverse mix of scientists, media, CEOs, and investors. The seats were packed, except for the top balcony. As Anne and Genne made their way upstairs, the two main speakers appeared on the stage.

The older gentleman was the world-renowned Dr. Bennett Bell, a Harvard professor, the head of Centre for Nanoscale Systems (CNS), and a long-time scholar of genetic engineering. He took his position on the left side of the stage, beside the statue of Josiah Quincy III, an eighteenth-century educator, politician, mayor of Boston, and president of Harvard University. Professor Bennett was in his early sixties. British by birth, he was recruited from Oxford to lead Harvard's Eugenics Department about ten years earlier. Although brilliant, he was very humble and quiet by nature. He rarely participated in spectacles such as these. His colleagues knew he agreed to this debate only from his own deep conviction about the topic. He gently placed his speaking notes on the podium, then patted his hair. He was feeling nervous due to all of the cameras and media attention. Teaching keen students seeking knowledge and talking to media seeking the next big story are two completely different things. His hands were shaking as his eyes combed through the audience. He ran his hands down an old, navy wool cardigan, then checked his shirt collar and bowtie. Finally, he forced his hands to come together in an awkward knot. He now stood still, waiting patiently for his opponent.

After a moment of commotion, the second speaker finally arrived. His appearance on the stage triggered a flood of whispers. Mannix Haldanne was a genetics pioneer and a strong advocate of eugenics. He was charismatic, cosmopolitan, ethnically ambiguous, drop-dead handsome, and sharply dressed, ready to take over the world. He was also extremely successful at the very young age of thirty-four. In 2030, Mannix discovered a way to alter the genetic code of various plants to revolutionize the construction industry. He developed a ground-breaking method of manufacturing new types of eco-friendly building materials. His materials were more flexible than plastic, more durable than steel, and extremely eco-friendly ... literally grown in special gardens. He cornered the market within two years and made billions. Then he used this money to revolutionize the energy market. He purchased several large international ocean waters in the Atlantic and Pacific from many surrounding countries giving them large undisclosed sums of money. He built large, incredibly expensive research and manufacturing facilities in the middle of the Atlantic and Pacific oceans, far from the shipping lanes, then invested his remaining money into further research. Within a year, he had genetically altered a specific type of deep-ocean plankton as the basis for, of all things, a high-capacity battery. Again, he cornered the market in two years. The batteries were lighter, had more capacity per volume, charged faster, were easier to manufacture, and, again, were very eco-friendly to produce as well as dispose of. Then, about four years ago, he disappeared. Just as dramatically, he surfaced only a few weeks ago with innovative ways to recode human genes to cure cancer, infertility, and even mental disorders.

Mannix knew this event would become a media frenzy and no doubt planned to use this event for promotional purposes. He knew how to make an entrance, arriving slightly late, then requesting to remove the podium on his side. This last-minute disturbance attracted just the attention he wanted. He then turned to the white statue located on his end of the stage, that of James Otis Jr., a statesman but also a revolutionary who advocated for U.S. separation from British rule. Mannix pretended to greet the statue and exchanged a few words, triggering a light chuckle from the crowd.

Mannix walked over to Professor Bell and shook his hand firmly but affectionately. He also bowed ever so slightly, no doubt as a sign of respect, and returned to his side of the stage.

Anna and Genne finally found a corner seat on the balcony about halfway down, directly in front of the elegant antique chandelier hanging low from the elaborate ceiling cupola. Cherry-colored wooden benches were not comfortable but they were very beautiful. In fact, almost every available space inside Sanders Theatre was covered by hand-carved decorative wood. Anna motioned to the wall behind the stage, where the top section was covered by large inscriptions in Latin. Genne smiled, but quickly refocused on the stage, eager to listen and learn.

Professor Bell motioned to the audience for quiet and to sit down. A few moments later, he opened with, "Welcome to you all, our most honored guests. Today's topic is deceptively simple: Is self-evolution, particularly genetic self-evolution, a personal freedom?" He then paused for a moment to allow this statement to sink into the audience.

Bell turned slightly to Mannix and continued, "And today we have the privilege to have both a pioneer, a revolutionary, and a mogul in the area of genetic engineering, Mannix Haldanne... A man who needs no introduction." Bell waited as an avalanche of applause filled the hall. Mannix returned the kindness of the audience with a charming smile and slight wave.

Bell waved with his hand for audience to settle and for clapping to finish, then continued, "Today we discuss whether a person has the liberty to self-evolve through genetic modification."

The few remaining whispers and noises extinguished quickly as Bell peered at the noisy parts of the audience, then proceeded, "We, as human beings, have basic rights including life, liberty, and the pursuit of happiness. We also have rights to promote our self-betterment through education and healthcare."

Bell paused then pointed to Mannix. "Dr. Haldanne will argue that these rights should be extended to genetic self-modification, a view I personally oppose." Again, he paused dramatically before proceeding, "I urge you to consider this topic carefully. No doubt it will attract the attention of media, politicians, lawyers, and scientists alike. Dr. Haldanne made sure of it with his latest research and innovations." He paused again before his final statement. "We can no longer deny that genetic engineering can alter our bodies, ours mind, and our lives. We must, however, decide if it is a freedom we are all entitled to or a risky, negligent experimentation we should avoid and prevent at all cost. We do not want to repeat what happened in China in 2015, when the government opened the floodgates to all types of genetic-engineering research. To this day, we're still paying the price for those experiments."

Bell lowered his voice. "Why don't you provide your opening statement, Dr. Haldanne?"

Mannix entered centre-stage with confidence. He stood silent for a moment then pulled his handkerchief from his breast pocket. He moved it in his hands quickly, then presented an apple. He took a small bite, then asked the audience, "How many of you eat apples? Please raise your hand." The room gradually filled with hands, some surprised by the question.

Mannix smiled and continued, "That's wonderful. Good for you. But did you know that approximately seventy percent of the apples sold in North American and European supermarkets today are genetically modified or have been cross-bred with other genetically modified apples?"

He raised the apple toward the crowd and spoke rapidly "The apple genome has been studied since 2010. Apples have seventeen chromosomes with more than fifty-seven thousand genes. Gene modification changes provide great benefits like bigger harvests, resilience to insects, and prolonged freshness."

He took another bite, chewed a bit, swallowed, smiled, and continued. "There are thousands of FDA-approved plants we now consume. Genetic alteration means specific genes are changed to achieve specific characteristics, for example preventing apples from browning. In most cases, no foreign DNA is introduced. We simply reprogram existing genes with new sequences. In rare cases, we introduce sequences from other plants.

"Tell me, was it morally wrong to genetically modify the apple?" He then added with a hint of sarcasm, looking at Bell, "Tell me, how dare we permit such an atrocity?" The audience began to whisper and snicker.

He continued his rhetorical inquisition. "Tell me, did the U.S. Congress vote on whether everyday people were allowed to consume genetically altered plants?"

He smiled with irony, then answered his own question "No. The FDA performed various scientific tests to establish the safety of the product. Then the consumers decided if they wanted to consume the product.

"There was no question of morality. It was a simply matter of science and choice."

He took another bite of the apple then placed it somewhat irrelevantly on Professor's Bell's podium. "Does a person have the right to self-evolve? Absolutely! Now, politicians and religious leaders will lead us to believe that the use of genetic modification is a question of morality and safety. They are simply afraid to admit it is a question of personal choice."

Bell interjected, offended by the apple and the last statement, "Dear sir, I am neither a politician nor a religious leader. I am a scientist and a scholar!"

Mannix stepped back, giving Bell centre stage. Bell continued, "In 2010, world-renowned geneticist Craig Venter announced to the world he was able to create synthetic life, the first self-reproducing self-functioning cell. But he did so, dear sir, in full cooperation and under the full scrutiny of Federal authorities."

Bell grabbed the half-eaten apple Mannix had left on the podium and continued, "The history of the human race is filled with violence. Eugenics first grew at the hand of World War II Nazis who recklessly pursued genetic experimentation with no concern for life. It is the responsibility of the government, based on scientific research, to distinguish which rights are safe and which ones should be prohibited.

"Genes are the building blocks of all organic life," he continued. "You cannot play with them like pieces of a transhumanist Lego house. They are far more complex. They affect each other and are dependent on each other. Altering genes is like removing a specific species from a complex ecosystem. The ecosystem will suffer and may even collapse altogether."

Bell climaxed with a visible grimace, "The research required to successfully map gene modification would require human testing. This testing may result in death. That is not a price this country or the science community is willing to pay, dear sir," then returned the apple into Mannix's hands. Embarrassed by his sudden display of emotion, he intentionally moved to the back of the stage.

"Dear Mr. Bell," Mannix responded. "Why overdramatize this matter? The FDA in the U.S., the same as its global counterparts in other countries, performs thorough tests to ensure the safety of any product. Products altered genetically are perceived no differently than the frozen dinner containing chemically modified corn components. FDA tests are scientific. They possess no personal bias and no religious beliefs. They simply focus on customer safety."

Professor Bell grimaced as Mannix referred to him as mister. He had dedicated the last forty-five years, the entirety of his professional life, to genetic science.

Mannix sensed Bell's frustration. He deliberately agitated him further, to his advantage. "Mr. Bell, thirty years ago most world governments did not permit the advanced genetic engineering used today. By their standards, you would be debunked as a scientist and fired from this fine institution. What response would you expect if, thirty years ago, you spoke in this same historic location about your work with Craig Venter to create synthetic life?"

Bell stepped forward and rushed his response. "Dear sir, do not compare your research of toying with complexity of human genetics with that of creating a single cell of synthetic life. That research took ten years and was executed in full compliance with both scientific and government regulatory bodies." Again Bell collected himself, regaining control, and relishing his next words. "At least we did not hide and perform our work in secret, as you have in the last few years Mr. Haldanne." He accentuated the last part in convenient verbal revenge.

Mannix's charming smile did not leave his face as he turned to his opponent. "I was not hiding, Professor Bell. Hiding implies fear of visibility or consequences. I have no such fear." He then turned back to the audience. "I was simply too busy understanding the beauty and complexity of human genetics ... a laborious effort I'm sure you understand ... and one that resulted in most fascinating discoveries." He paused, then, "Professor Bell, perhaps you are the one that is afraid. You have yet to answer my question."

Bell's answer was reluctant, but honest. "It is no surprise humanity fears what they do not understand. You are correct. Thirty years ago, the science of human genetics was quite immature. Creating synthetic life was perceived as dangerous, unethical, and immoral. But humanity has learned a lot in the last thirty years. We now have a much greater insight and appreciation of the science involved." He turned toward the audience. "This also includes an appreciation of its risks and limitations." His deep, wise eyes stared out at the audience, creating another dramatic pause.

Mannix took centre-stage again, filling the silence Bell left in the crowd. "Of all people, Professor Bell, I would expect you to understand what I am doing. I dare you to join the spirit of Robert Oppenheimer, who once spoke in this very room. He once said, 'See things as they might be, not as you believe they are.'" He then took another bite of the apple and posed another question to the crowd. "Does anyone know how many chromosomes a human being has?" A few people in the audience raised their hands and shouted numbers.

Mannix scanned the crowd. He didn't want to engage someone from the media or business. He noticed a tall man in the back wearing a worn-out raincoat. He looked sceptical, but genuinely curious about the topic. He pointed and called out to him as the man's lips quietly provided the correct answer. "You, sir! By the door in the raincoat! What was your answer?"

The unshaven men looked out of place and surprised at the attention he was getting. He quietly said, "Twenty-three pairs of chromosomes," as if he wanted to be ignored.

Mannix snatched the answer and drove it home. "That's right: twenty-three pairs for a total of forty-six chromosomes. Let's compare that to the apple's seventeen chromosomes. The difference may not feel substantial. However, when dealing with genetic complexity, I believe the difference is exponential. Let me show you."

Mannix then did something unexpected. He reached into his side jacket pocket, took out a strange round device, and then threw it into the air in the middle of the hall. The item paused in midair, just under the chandelier, and began to project various images filling the space above the crowd. The clarity and quality of the three-dimensional imagery was spellbinding. Mannix scanned the audience with satisfaction at seeing them completely enraptured. He jumped down to the audience level and walked to the middle of the aisle, pointing to different objects being displayed. "Ladies and gentlemen, Dr. Bell is arguing quite eloquently that we must first understand something before we can build it. Yet I believe with all of my heart that the opposite is true. I join Richard Feynman in saying 'What I cannot build, I cannot understand.' I have not spent the last few years in hiding. I invested it. I completely committed and consumed myself with building a new foundation for human genetic engineering." He let the last statement hang in the air as the hall filled with whispers.

Mannix continued. "Let's use a mathematical proxy to show this difficult challenge." He projected a visualization of an apple genome and said, "Let's represent the apple's genetic complexity using a number two to the power of seventeen ... seventeen, of course, referring to the number of chromosomes. That equals 131,072. It's a nice six-digit number." He then smiled widely, waved his hand, and projected a visualization of the human genome. "In comparison, human genetic complexity can be represented using the number two to the power of forty-six. That equals to much larger 70,368,744,177,664." He motioned with his hand again. The two numbers moved side by side and then morphed into spheres, allowing a visual comparison between the volume of the two spheres. He pointed and said, "This difference was immense," accentuating the last part of the statement. The smaller projected sphere began to shrink, until it became a tiny dot and faded altogether. He then snapped his fingers and all of the dazzling projections disappeared.

Mannix dramatically walked back on to the stage speaking softly, almost philosophically. "I concur with Dr. Bell. The understanding and altering of the human genome would be madness

…" He spoke slowly, almost stretching the next words, "… madness, unless …" His speech accelerated, "… unless we don't think of them as individual genes." He snapped his fingers again, and the human genome once reappeared, bright and magnified in front of everyone. "We already know genes cannot be altered individually. Many affect each other and are dependent on one another." He then pointed to an area on the helix that began to glow. "Imagine for a moment we could understand human genes in sets. This grouping would greatly decrease the level of complexity we have to understand and manage."

Dr. Bell interceded, genuinely amazed and curious. "How significantly, Mannix?"

Mannix turned to him and smiled, as if he had expected the question and relished providing an answer. "My dear Dr. Bell, if we are to continue using our mathematical proxy … it would be represented by a number of two to the power of twenty-three or 8,388,608." He paused to let people reach their own epiphanies, then finished with, "A mere digit more than the apple genome." He then snapped his fingers twice. All of the projections disappeared, and the round device flew down and into his hand. Mannix quickly walked back to the stage, picked up the half-eaten apple, pocketed both, and waited for chaos to ensue.

Almost simultaneously, a flurry of photos and questions came from the audience. They were anything from, "Have you done any human experimentation?" to "Can this cure cancer?" to "How dare you alter God's holy creation?"

Mannix raised his hands to calm the crowd. As they settled, he conceded, "I will tell you three things, and then I really have to go." He raised his hand to show one finger. "Yes this technology can cure cancer, diabetes, hair loss, infertility, and a lot more." He raised his second finger. "I am not talking about something hypothetical. Human trials have been running, although secretly, for two years now. Yes, they were monitored by various governments and with the full consent of the participants. They were performed on those who most needed it, the terminally ill and in some countries death-row prisoners." He then showed his third finger. "Today marks the day this technology is revealed for public use. In fact, I'm meeting the first candidate for their genetic enhancement immediately after this session." Despite shouts and questions, he wrapped up with, "You'll hear a lot more about this in days to come. Now I really must be going. It was great to see you all."

Mannix disappeared through the backstage entrance as quickly as he had appeared. Several people attempted to follow, but were quickly intercepted by security. The floor turned into a frenzy of media trying to contact Mannix-owned companies, scholars discussing the merits of this new technology, business people considering the new opportunities this would create, doctors debating the impact such a procedure would have on participants' health, and those who questioned the morality of such treatments.

Chapter 2: A New Beginning

"Are you Genne and Anne Manning?" a voice greeted them as they finally managed to navigate out of busy Memorial Hall.

Anne's eyes met those of a tall, beautiful, dark-haired woman and responded "Yes, we are."

The woman extended her hand and stated confidently, "My name is Innes. Please follow me to your appointment." She then motioned to a black limo parked on the street.

Genne responded, "Pleasure to meet you, Innes. Please lead the way."

As they followed, Anne could not help but admire the woman. She was a little over six feet tall, probably in her mid-thirties, and thin, but visibly fit. She was wearing a green blouse and short blue skirt, with a yellow scarf and red high-heeled shoes. All of the colors were strong but earthy and mixed together very well. She also wore a multi-colored bracelet made of fabric and a wooden ring. Her profile was striking. She had very strong facial features. Her oval eyes were accented with black eye liner hugging the eye lashes and spilling sharply outward, almost cat-like. Her nose was round, of proportionate width, and hanging quite low, almost to her narrow, but full lips. She spoke elegantly, pronouncing words almost poetically, and with a slight accent. Her movements were graceful and controlled.

As they arrived at the limo, Innes opened the door, met Genne's eyes, and spoke with calm, but clear, directness, "Please understand, everything about this session is to be held with utmost secrecy. Failure to do so will automatically disqualify you from moving forward with any procedures."

"Of course," Genne responded, and Anne agreed with a nod. Innes smiled ever-so-slightly in acknowledgment, then opened the limo door wide. She followed Anne and Genne into the rear of the oversized limo. It was big enough to fit twenty people. The interior was modern and luxurious. Anne was surprised that she couldn't recognize the materials. Instead of typical mahogany and leather, the interior of the car was fitted with a single uniform material. The closest thing she could compare it to was white coral. Yet this material was far softer and comfortably melded to their bodies. As they sat down, they saw Mannix sitting on the opposite side. He motioned them to move closer to him. As they settled, the limo began to move.

Mannix jumped right in. "Welcome, Genne and Anne. It's so wonderful to finally meet you. What did you think of today's presentation?"

Genne responded quietly, still processing everything, "Simply remarkable." After a moment of awkward silence, he rushed to add, "I'm just wondering how you found us."

"It's quite simple Genne," Mannix replied. "It's your genes." He smiled as if intending the pun, then continued. "You recently did some genetic screening. I believe you were simply curious." He placed his hand on Genne's shoulder, "As most people do, you seek to discover any serious disease predispositions you may have." Genne exchanged looks with Anne as Mannix proceeded. "I recently acquired the company you used for these tests." Mannix looked directly at Genne. "You have a very unique genome. One that's optimal for a genetic enhancement procedure I've developed. Innes, my colleague, contacted you last week, inviting you to the debate as well as this very meeting." He motioned with his open hand. "Of course, we'll be providing you with a full report on the genetic screening you requested," then leaned further forward and added dramatically, "I do, however, have a life-altering proposal for you."

As if on cue, Innes served warm aromatic, full-bodied, and perfectly brewed chai. Anne took a sip, and asked, "If we understand the situation correctly, there is nothing physically wrong with Genne. You are however interested in somehow … improving his genes?" She grimaced, "I'm not sure I understand."

"Yes," Mannix reassured. "Your husband's genes are completely normal." He then looked to Genne. "I am not talking about fixing something that's broken. I'm talking about creating something magnificent on the solid foundation that you already are." He looked directly into Genne's eyes and continued, "I simply want to alter your genes to make you … far more than you ever thought you could be."

Seeing that his visitors remained cautious and concerned, Mannix continued, "Imagine being stronger mentally, smarter, more determined, and more confident, having high metabolism, being in great physical shape, and so much more." He waited for his words to sink in. "Once you understand the procedure, you will, of course, judge its safety for yourself and decide whether to proceed with it. You will be provided with everything, including the very best recovery healthcare, completely free. The primary thing we are interested in is the ability to publicize your procedure and its results." Another dramatic pause was followed by, "I want to give you a new life Genne, one you can't even imagine."

Mannix shifted his attention to include Anne. "Please stay in Boston for the weekend. Innes made all of the arrangements. She will bring you back to my office on Monday. I know you need time to process and discuss my offer." He then added, "I want you to know this is a tested, reliable procedure, not just science fiction."

The limo stopped. Innes quickly whisked Mr. and Mrs. Manning out of the vehicle, right into front entrance of the Omni Parker House, one of Boston's landmark hotels. Mannix and the limo moved off as Innes took them inside. She briefed them as they entered the grand lobby "You will be staying on the fourteenth floor. Your belongings were already moved there from your current hotel." She smiled elegantly, "Your accommodations, dining, and admission to various attractions have been generously paid for by Dr. Mannix."

The group was greeted by three different hotel staff, including a young busboy. Innes bowed slightly to say goodbye, "I will pick you both up at two p.m. on Monday. Till then, please do enjoy yourself and think about the proposal." They were totally astounded by this turn of events. In the commotion of attendants greeting them, they didn't even notice which door she exited through.

Chapter 3: Suspicious Circumstances

Agent Glenn Abbot reclined at his desk. In one hand he was holding a half-eaten burger, in the other one, a file about a murder. *Why is the FBI investigating a common murder?* he thought. He scratched his rugged, unshaven face and took another bite of cholesterol-filled beefy goodness. Glenn was not exactly a life success story. He was, however, a solid, reliable agent. His parents had left him when he was three. He moved between foster homes till he was fifteen, then ran away and lived on the streets of Chicago. There he picked up some nasty habits and a few really bad friends. Thankfully, a kind cop befriended him after he overdosed on street drugs. Glenn grew up to be cynical, distrusting all people except for very few he really admired. He also carried a hatred for himself, internalizing that his parents abandoned him. As he grew up he turned to books, both to lose himself and to catch up on his missed schooling. He excelled in biology, physics, mathematics, and law. He graduated from college then St. George's University with honors, despite working crazy hours to pay for his own education and a small apartment on Chicago's south side. He had some difficulty finding fulfilling work and, in his early twenties, reached a point of disillusionment. He constantly failed to meet his own high moral standards. Following his mentor's example and endorsement, he applied to the FBI and was accepted. Being an FBI agent was his path to redemption, and he was damned good at it. He had street smarts, great instincts, and sheer brilliance. He was relentless and highly effective, and his life was going well. He met a beautiful woman, a high-school teacher, and they married just before he turned thirty. Unfortunately, his work soon consumed him and his relationship suffered. Two months earlier, after much conflict and a restraining order, he was divorced and now was living in his ancient car.

Another agent passed by his desk, dropping a friendly remark, "Hey Glenn, your house is still parked outside. When are you renovating the bathroom?"

Glenn grimaced, then fired back, smiling, "Your wife didn't mind it last night, Jack." He then looked up at the passing agent and continued, "And I don't need a bathroom. I've been crapping in your toilet for the last few weeks."

Jack had apparently expected this kind of comeback and laughed gregariously. Pausing beside Glenn, Jack continued, "You're still coming for dinner tonight, right? Janet is cooking

Italian. But none of this dirty talk in front of her. She would kill me if she knew we talk about her this way."

Glenn grinned. "Of course I'm coming, and I really appreciate the offer." He continued softly, almost to himself, "Living in a car is great for your bank account, but terrible for your morale and your diet."

Glenn finished his burger and returned to his reading, searching his messy desk for another file, this one entitled GPRP, an acronym for Genetic Prisoner Reform Program. He dove right into the contents. About two years ago, a biotech company owned by Mannix developed a genetic program for behavior modification of extremely violent inmates. This technology was highly successful in isolating and modifying the so-called *violence gene* in inmates with double Y chromosomes. Many of these prisoners were serving life sentences without chance of parole and caused numerous problems for prisons. Mannix had also apparently developed other procedures, to modify the addiction gene and treat hereditary compulsive tendencies. The FBI file was curiously missing numerous level-four, highly classified documents, but Glenn had enough information to establish a general understanding of these treatments. These procedures were unusually successful, allowing inmates to quickly reintegrate back into the prison community. The prisoners who underwent the gene modification exhibited remarkable changes, and they became positive contributors to the prison community. Some performed so well that they earned parole and now lived normal lives.

Why is FBI investigating a common murder case? he asked himself again, switching back to the case file. This particular murder was by a prisoner who had undergone the genetic-modification procedure. Glenn grew more frustrated as he studied the details. Former prisoner John Doe was one of the first to undergo the treatment. In fact, he volunteered after years of being haunted by visions of his multiple rape victims. His improvement was very rapid and radical. Just a year after the treatment he was released on parole. He took a job as a bookkeeper. He had apparently been adjusting to his new life quite well. He rented an apartment and spent his weekends reading books. He wore a monitoring bracelet and checked in weekly with both his parole officer and his GPRP specialist.

Glenn moaned. The murderer's real name was replaced by the anonymous John Doe to keep the real name classified. "Another John Doe. He really gets around," he muttered. He wondered if the name was even material. Many prisoners changed their names when trying to start over. He continued reading. A few moments later, an uncomfortable feeling settled deep in his stomach. Something didn't add up. John Doe's fingerprints were found all over a brutal murder scene, including the murder weapon. The victim was chopped into pieces and their body parts used to paint on a large apartment wall, "The hell with the rabbits." The file showed the jagged writing in blood. Glenn whispered to himself, "He is a bad painter. Blood red totally doesn't match that couch or the carpet." Then he thought about the message, "What's wrong with rabbits, anyway?" He strained to recall the same phrase in a classical literary piece.

The victim was a nobody, a female accountant in a small company that manufactured common plumbing parts. There was nothing unique or particular about the victim. She lived a normal and quiet life, thirty-one years old, never married, spent her days at home, enjoyed classical music, no known addictions, jogged every morning, no unusual purchases recently, no strange family history. There seem to be no obvious motive for the murder. There seemed to be no connection between the victim and the murderer. The victim wasn't raped. Glenn sighted in frustration. "Mr. Doe, my day today would have been much better if you simply tried dating her instead."

He kept reading until he landed on something he hadn't expected. Apparently, after savagely killing and dismembering the victim, the murderer went to the bathroom, sat in a bathtub reading Steinbeck's classic *Of Mice and Men*, and painted the bathroom red with his brains and a double-barreled shotgun. Glenn sighed. *First he painted the living room then he redecorated the bathroom. Both a mess.*" The last scene didn't make any sense. First, John Doe had no history of using weapons in any of his previous crimes. Second, why bring a classic hard-cover book with you if you're going to commit suicide, even if it was by a Nobel-winning writer? Third, why commit suicide in the victim's bathroom? Glenn wrote down the name Lennie Small, one of two main characters in Steinbeck's book, a violent and mentally disabled man unaware of the horrors he caused. He studied photos of the bathroom and noticed that John Doe's eyes were two different colors. He wondered if that mattered, then mentally parked that detail for later. *But where is George in all of this?* he wondered, referring to the other main character of the book, a small man who befriended, guarded, and occasionally covered up Lenny's messes.

Glenn became uneasy. The timing of this crime, at the precipice of Mannix's debate and the announcement he attended earlier that day, was not coincidental. The scene was too convenient, a classic orgy of evidence where all of the evidence to solve the case is provided in the crime scene. If the circumstances of the murder were made public, especially related to Mannix's Genetic Prisoner Reform Program, the media would have a frenzy with both Mannix and the federal agency that allowed and monitored this program. *No doubt this program is precisely why the FBI is involved,* he thought. *The federal government does like to keep its reputation clean, and would choose to investigate this quietly, in-house.*

He instinctively focused on John Doe. *Let's follow Lenny. Perhaps we'll find George.* He knew from experience that the agency wanted him to pursue and question the suspicious crime scene. At the same time, Glenn had his own agenda. He didn't trust the agency, especially with the withheld level-four documents. He would simultaneously pursue his own investigation into the prisoner program. That's where his gut was leading him.

The first thing he needed to know is who John Doe really was. He looked at the only note he had written so far, Lenny Small, and thought to himself *Could it be that easy?* He proceeded to search federal databases for any prisoners in the last five years with that name. It was a long shot, but two names appeared, one in California and one in Massachusetts. He quickly read the latter's file and thought, *Too easy*, finding that the personal details matched quite well. He wrote down the sentencing details, list of closest friends, and last-known address. Then he smiled. "Mr. John Doe, I hereby rename you to Lenny Small."

He switched focus and looked up the primary contact for the Genetic Prisoner Reform Program. He recognized the location, on the South Boston Naval Annex. He knew he would need permission to enter the naval base. He submitted an electronic requisition, which he knew he would not receive until the morning. He noted the address, grabbed his raincoat, and left the office with one thought stuck in his head, *Why is the office for a small biotech and genetics company located on a U.S. naval base?*

Chapter 4: History in the Making

Anne sat in a luxurious armchair, still in shock. *Harvey Parker Suite at the historic Parker House.* A hotel brochure told her that many famous people, including Charles Dickens and JFK, had stayed in this very room. She ran her finger over the desk looking for dust but found none. *Historic and spotless*, she thought.

Genne crashed on the bed, still wearing his shoes. "Remarkable. Just remarkable. You live through your quiet, normal life and right out of nowhere you get smacked in the face with the opportunity of a lifetime."

Anne noticed a small black package on the table with an elegant embossed blue H+ logo. Curious, she began opening it. Genne got up and joined her. Inside was a spherical device similar to the one Mannix had used during the debate. When Anne touched it, the object began hovering in the middle of the room and projected a scene. Four visible projectors were placed equal distance from each other, while other sensors and speakers weren't as visible. Genne wasn't sure how the device floated in the air without any noise. "I wonder how this toy works," he said.

The device answered in a warm, but child-like voice. "Genne and Anne Manning recognized." The sphere began to turn and blink. "No other parties or recording devices present. Knowledge database unlocked." It then invited, "How may I help you? Please state your question."

Anne sat down on the couch closer to the device and asked, "What information do you have?"

The sphere projected a long list of topics and answered, "I can provide information regarding genetic-enhancement technology, impact on health, and the procedure itself, as well as connect you directly to H+ offices."

Genne got right to the point. "What can this type of treatment improve or change?"

The device projected a series of images as it ran through various scenarios. "In the case of a life-debilitating disease, the procedure can completely reverse or eliminate it. Current treatments can eradicate common types of cancer, diabetes, infertility, addiction, depression, lupus, and many other conditions. The same technology can be used to enhance a person's current abilities including metabolism, muscle strength, energy level, confidence, focus, memory, recall, IQ level, life span, and more."

Anne shook her head in disbelief.

Genne pondered for a moment then asked, "How does the procedure work?"

The device projected the image of a white cocoon, then explained, "The procedure takes place in a secure facility and takes approximately twenty-four hours. The patient is placed in a specialized FM2030 pod that both modifies genetic material and ensures that life signs remain stable. The technology used to modify a patient's genetic material during the procedure is classified. Full recovery takes four to six weeks, depending on the complexity of genetic changes and the patient's motivation."

"What impact does this procedure have on the body? Are there any risks or side effects?" Anne asked.

The sphere didn't project anything. Instead it spoke, "The treatment has a one hundred percent survival rate. There are no known physical side effects, such as damage to organs, infections, or secondary diseases. The procedure is non-invasive, and it leaves no wounds or scarring."

Genne interrupted, "Then why does recovery take so long if it's non-invasive?"

The device responded, "The recovery time is not required for any type of physical healing. However, the patients do undergo significant personal change, resulting in a shock. They often form a new identity based on their changed abilities and / or the absence of disease, like cancer. The recovery time is required for the patient to mentally adapt to who they have become."

Anne noticed Genne was still processing the info so she asked, "Was this procedure performed on other people?"

The sphere responded, "Federally approved human test trials have been running for more than two years now. Initial subjects included terminally ill patients as well as life-sentence prisoners."

Genne followed up on Anne's line of questioning with, "How about normal people like me?"

The device paused for a moment, then responded, "You are the first potential human subject without any pre-conditions. Secondary subjects have been identified and will be contacted if you choose to decline this offer."

Anne then asked, "Why did you choose us?"

The Device responded, "Sorry, but I do not have this information."

Genne asked, "Where does this procedure take place?"

The sphere again beeped and responded, "The exact location of the secure facility is classified."

Genne looked at Anne and said, "I think I'm done for now. Already a lot to think about. How about you, honey?"

Anne was equally fazed and needed to process the information. "I'm good."

The sphere returned to its base, saying, "Thank you for your questions. You can reactivate me by touching me and asking additional questions."

Anne and Genne decided today was enough for a year's worth of their lives They were emotionally drained. They ordered room service, and took turns showering. Genne began to reflect as Anne went to shower first. He was just a normal marketing manager in his forties. No kids, a choice they made together to travel and enjoy life instead. Average build, average grades, and average life. The only unique thing about him was his first name, misspelled on his birth certificate. He wondered if that's precisely what Mannix wanted, just an average guy he could turn into something far more. *That's exactly how a showman demonstrates to the world how great his technology is.*

It's not that Genne didn't want more. He was quite successful at marketing. His marriage was strong. *I guess there is always room for improvement,* he thought. With his midlife crisis creeping up, the idea of being something more sounded very enticing. He was getting complacent and bored, even stuck. He didn't want to admit it, but he did want more. He had hoped to be so much more than he was right now. The prospect of being a genetic-modification pioneer excited him. The idea of overcoming his long-time weaknesses and shortcomings awakened a new hope and courage inside him. His life would finally have more meaning.

As he was thinking, Anne showered slowly, soaping and lathering various parts of her body. Her regimen included compulsively and carefully washing from head to toe, one body part at a time, making sure she felt totally clean. She reflected on the ritual, thinking it was almost obsessive, but then followed it anyway. She switched to worrying about her husband. She loved him and wanted the best for him. More importantly, she wanted him to make the right choice, one that would stand the test of time.

She moved on to meeting Innes today. That woman was so confident, strong, fit, and beautiful. Her clothing was vibrant and elegant. She spoke with great intelligence and class. In many ways, Anne wished she could be more like Innes. She wondered how exciting it would be to work with Mannix, instead of at her current, boring job as a junior editor at a small local newspaper.

Genne knocked on the bathroom door and called, "Food just arrived." Anne mentally reviewed the progress of her washing ritual. She was down to her feet, but quite caught up in her thoughts. She worried, naturally, what would happen to Genne when he changed. Would she get a new and enhanced husband 2.0, or more than she bargained for? Would he still want her the way she was, lacking the improvements he received? As she finished and shut the water off, she was distracted by the engraved bathtub, multi-directional shower head, and silky towel she held in her hands. Her thoughts returned, and she cursed herself for being such a scatterbrain. She joked to herself, *No doubt Mannix purposefully chose a man. Men are simple: food, sleep, sex and they're fine. Finding a cure for a woman's fragmented brain, hormones, and emotions was far too difficult,* then she grinned and continued, *That's because women are already enhanced!* Another thought came as she put on her robe, *I wonder if he can cure PMS?*

Anne entered the living room, finding her husband already eating and enjoying himself. He spoke with his mouth partly full, "Hon, looks like Mannix ordered a few extras on our behalf: lobster, caviar, and champagne. And you have to try this tuna carpaccio with avocado salad. Everything tastes awesome, and the city view through the window is amazing!"

They chatted for a while trying and enjoying the different foods. They temporarily distracted themselves by planning various weekend activities. They knew Monday would come quickly, but after twelve years of marriage they already sensed each other's thoughts and perspectives.

Chapter 5: Round One

"I will need to check your car, sir," said the armed guard at the entrance to the South Boston Navy Base.

"Are you sure you want to do that?" Glenn replied, looking at the back seat full of junk and clothing.

The soldier rolled his eyes and said, "I have to do it sir, regardless of your FBI clearance. Your papers say you will be visiting the H+. That's a private facility. Please pull over to the left, unlock your trunk, and step out of the vehicle."

Glenn proceeded as the guard instructed, grabbed his coffee, and stood by as the guard examined his vehicle. He figured maybe he could get some info in the meantime. He checked the nametag and rank on his uniform and said, "What's your first name Lieutenant Thompson?"

The guard looked back at him, slightly annoyed, opened the trunk wide, and responded "Lieutenant Thompson should do just fine, Agent Abbot." He dove into the trunk, filled with suitcases, shoes, and strange personal artefacts. "Would you mind explaining why an FBI agent is driving a rusty, twelve-year-old Dodge Charger? And what's with all these suitcases? Are you relocating or something?"

Glenn was quick to justify the situation. "It's complicated. Divorce ...." He then decided to cut the story short. "Enough said.

This is my personal car. I would rather drive this mechanical lady then get an unmarked loaner from the agency."

The guard lifted the base of the trunk to check if anything was stored with the spare tire. "Why would you choose this rust bucket over an agency car?"

"Hey, don't talk about her like that. Sure, she's got years and miles on her, but her heart is tried and true," he responded, annoyed. "She's never let me down, which is far more than I can say for my ex-wife."

Lieutenant Thompson moved to check the back seat. "Understood. Sorry to hear about the divorce…" then rushed on, in partial shock. "Wait, are you actually living in this car?"

Glenn tried to evade the question. "Primarily storing my belongings till I find more permanent accommodations."

The guard rolled his eyes and moved to the front, checking under the seats and in the glove compartment. "Not finding any weapons or illegal substances. That's good. Please open the hood."

Glenn popped the hood, lifted it, and asked, "Hey, why would a private facility be located on a U.S. Navy base?"

The guard paused to look Agent Abbot in the eyes. "I don't know sir. I just got transferred from Seattle. Shouldn't this be something the FBI already knows?"

"Sure, but I'm not buying the official answer I'm getting."

The guard examined a few gaps around the chassis but found nothing. "Guys say it has been here for more than a year. It's off limits to most military personnel. Sorry, but I don't really know much more." He then stepped back and said, "You're good to go, sir."

Glenn closed the hood, then proceeded to reorganize his trunk. He stretched the ordeal to probe a bit further. "Would you mind telling me if they get any interesting visitors?"

Thompson paused, considering what to disclose "Not sure I should tell you…" After a moment, he relented. "The strangest thing they get are high-security prisoner transfer trucks." He quickly added, "Now, please stop asking me questions. You are working for the agency, aren't you?"

Glenn got into his car and restarted it. "Lieutenant Thompson, thank you for your assistance."

The guard walked away, raising his hand goodbye. "Good to meet you, Agent Abbot. Please follow the H+ signs to get to the facility. I'll let them know you're coming. And please, get a locker or something for all your crap. It's really embarrassing."

Glenn drove about two minutes, then approached a secondary gate. Security cameras pointed to his face and his license plates. A nearby speaker screeched "ID please." He rolled down the window to show his well-worn FBI credentials. The gate opened as the speaker directed, "Park in visitor parking on the far side of the building." Glenn drove forward, circled around the building, and pulled into first spot in an empty visitor parking lot. He stepped out and took a look at the modern, twelve-storey glass building. He entered the main lobby and immediately noticed high security walls and non-military guards. He walked up to the main desk and handed over his permission to enter the facility. One of the armed guards said, "Agent Abbot, we rarely get visitors here, especially on Saturday morning, so let's skip the pleasantries. What is your business here?"

Glenn hadn't expected a warm welcome. He stopped examining the building, looked back at the guard, and responded, "Murder investigation. I called ahead to set up a meeting with your firm's representative."

The guard handed back the paper, pulled out a plastic tray, then pointed sharply and said, "Leave all weapons, wallet, jacket, all metals, all liquids, and your shoes with me. Then have a seat in that waiting area. Someone will be with you shortly."

Glenn was surprised at this level of security for a biotech company but didn't want to push back on his first visit. He did as directed. The guard took the tray to the wall, entered a code, and the tray disappeared behind a small, locked gate.

Glenn sat down, feeling somewhat naked without his badge, gun, and com device. He also noticed a small hole in his left sock, right above the big toe. He crossed his ankles to hide this unprofessional sight. Then he returned to examining the interior of the building. He realized that most of the building was made of a wood-like substance and a translucent, plastic-like material, no doubt invented or at least genetically engineered by Mannix. He saw no signs of metal, steel, or iron, even for the elevators. On the rear wall he noticed a quote overshadowing the lobby, *The human species can, if it wishes, transcend itself,* credited to Julian Huxley, a British evolutionary biologist. He moved his attention to the guards. They must have been ex-military, probably Navy Seals. It was obvious from their routine, language, and how they carried themselves. They were wearing bulletproof vests and carried FN SCAR-16 assault rifles as well as M9 Beretta pistols. Not anything he wanted to mess with. He saw someone walking out of the elevator, and turned his attention to her.

A sharply dressed woman passed the security area and approached him, "My name is Innes Tannah. Please follow me to a secure area."

"I'm Agent Abbot. Please lead the way." Glenn followed her to a secluded room, directly adjacent to the lobby. It had no exits except the door they had entered from, right next to the security desk. It was quite plain with a few business armchairs and a strange, single-piece legless oval coffee table. Innes pointed Glenn to a seat and waved as the door closed automatically behind them.

She got right to the point. "I understand the FBI is investigating a sensitive murder investigation. How can we be of service?"

Glenn sat up in the chair, "I really appreciate you making time for me on the weekend. I was hoping to ask you a few questions about the Prisoner Reform Program."

Innes smiled softly and replied, "Yes, I understand that your main suspect was previously part of our program and underwent a genetic behavior-modification procedure. What would you like to know?"

Glenn was curious about Innes. "Would you mind telling me what your role in the company is?"

Innes answered quickly, "I am one of the GPRP program administrators here at H+."

"How long have you worked here and what's the nature of your work?"

Innes forced an impatient smile. "I've worked here for two years and the nature of my work is frankly none of your business. I don't believe you're investigating me." She crossed her hands and added, "Why don't you get right to the point, Agent Abbot?"

Glenn looked directly into her eyes, searching for any movement. "I'm curious about the procedure. How does it work? How effective is it? How successful was it on this specific patient?"

Innes's eyes didn't flicker. She stared back with strength and confidence. "Unfortunately, the details of the procedure are highly classified, and above your level of clearance. I can tell you the same information we already provided to the FBI and other federal agencies. The patient in question did undergo the treatment approximately two years ago. The procedure was so effective that he was released from prison on parole and reintegrated back into society. We monitor all of our patients remotely. His last check in two weeks ago showed no signs of behavior degradation. In fact, the patient continued to improve."

Glenn got the feeling he was outwitted and outgunned in the current line of questioning. It seemed Innes already knew far more than he did, and clearly didn't want to share any of it. Perhaps she was already monitoring the investigation. Perhaps she was even monitoring his progress. "I visited the suspect's apartment last night." Glenn was, in fact, planning to visit Lenny's apartment in the next few days. He continued, "I found nothing special. He was, however, an avid reader. Did you know what kind of books he loved reading?"

Innes paused, then recovered quickly and answered, "Yes, he did love reading. It was one of the recovery tactics we introduced. I believe he loved travel books. He did have plans to travel around the world. Why do you ask?"

"Did you know he was found with a book at the murder scene?"

Innes responded, irritated, "I'm not sure why you are asking me about details of your investigation."

Glenn retracted, trying another angle, "My apologies. Would it be possible for me to interview any other patients that have undergone a similar treatment?... perhaps friends or cellmates of Lenny?"

This time Innes was ready and didn't flinch at hearing the name that was concealed in the case files. She replied, coldly, "Of course we will assist with the investigation in any way we can. Let me see what I can do. I'll send you information on Monday morning."

"Do you believe this murder was an intentional plot to undermine Mannix's recent announcement?" he asked.

Innes returned a charming smile. "Isn't that why the FBI is involved? Yes, Mannix's ideals have many enemies. Perhaps that is one mystery you can solve and share with us, Agent Abbot."

Glenn decided to ask his final question "There's another thing. Why is a private biotech company located on a highly secure U.S. Navy base?"

Innes met his eyes sharply then got up, opened the door, and gestured with her hand for Glenn to exit. "Agent Abbot, you know better than to ask this question."

Glenn persisted, "I mean your genetic research must be of interest to a number of federal agencies, including the military ..."

Innes maintained her professional air. "I'm afraid you are outstaying your welcome, Agent Abbot." She stepped out of the room and motioned to her security detail.

Glenn noticed, got up, and followed her. "One more question. Why are Lenny's eyes different color? His health and prison records state he had green eyes till your procedure."

Innes closed the door behind him and said "Goodbye, Agent Abbot" with cold indifference and began to Walk away.

"Maybe coffee next time?" Glenn joked.

Innes turned around for a moment to meet his eyes. "I hope, for both of our sakes, that we don't meet again." She stepped behind the security station and got onto the elevator, leaving Glenn in the lobby.

Glenn approached the security desk. The guard was all ready with his belongings.

"She is kind of hot" Glenn tried, trying to get some kind of facial response from the armed guard. All he got back was a cold stare and blink.

Glenn mumbled, while putting on his shoes, "Maybe she doesn't dig guys in uniform." Again, there was no response from the guard.

"Right, still grumpy from this morning," Glenn left the lobby, got into his car, and drove away, thinking *I wonder if their attitude is a job requirement or just how they like to treat uninvited guests.*

Chapter 6: The Interview

The limousine's windows were thick and tinted, no doubt bulletproof. Again, Genne and Anne Manning had no way of knowing where Innes was taking them. They knew they were still in Boston, about twenty minutes from their hotel, and that they had been driven through city traffic. The vehicle went down a ramp before stopping. The doors opened inside a large parking garage and Innes escorted them to an unusual elevator: no buttons, glass walls, and virtually no noise.

Anne broke the silence. "I love that bracelet you are wearing. I saw it Friday."

Innes responded, "Thank you. It's from Cairo."

Anne continued, "Oh, are you Egyptian? I can't quite pinpoint your background."

Innes replied, reluctantly obliging Anne's curiosity, "Egyptian on my mother's side, Japanese on my father's."

"Must have been interesting growing up," Genne remarked. "Very different cultures."

Once again Innes responded succinctly, signaling she did not wish to talk about her personal life, "Indeed."

The elevator arrived at its destination. She led the way on to a massive penthouse floor. The layout was extraordinary. The walls, floors, and ceiling were partly translucent, made of a plastic-like, green material. The same material continued from the floor to form a large S-shaped table, about thirty feet long. On both ends, the surface lowered as it swung about, to form a sitting surface. Nowhere else had they seen furniture even remotely resembling this.

Innes led them to one end of the table. "Please do sit down. I have a few formalities I want to go through before Dr. Haldanne arrives."

As Anne and Genne sat down, Innes circled around the table. A seat literally grew from the floor, allowing her to sit directly in front of them.

"Did you enjoy your stay here in Boston?" she asked courteously.

Anne replied joyously, "Oh, yes. The hotel and food were wonderful. Please pass my thanks to Mannix … I mean Dr. Haldanne."

Innes looked up with a slight smile. "If you don't mind, he really prefers if you call him Mannix." She continued, "Do you have any questions about the procedure?"

Genne smiled and said, "Your crystal ball gadget answered most of our questions. It's just that…" he paused, stuck.

"Yes?" Innes coaxed.

Anne jumped in, "Well, it's nothing like we've done before. It's unprecedented. We understand there is a lot you cannot tell us, some of it for our safety. It's just difficult to make a decision like this …"

Genne spoke into the silence, "That's a pretty cool device."

Innes smiled, "Yes, it's one of Mannix's inventions."

She focused on Genne now. "And I'm assuming you reviewed the contract and wish to go ahead with the procedure. Unfortunately, we cannot allow you to involve a lawyer. It would breach our confidentiality clause …" Then she added, with a barely noticeable eye roll "… and no lawyer would be equipped to handle this case."

Genne looked at Anne, then back at Innes, and finally replied. "I understand. Of course… enhance me." He hesitated over his choice of words, then rushed on, "It's definitely an opportunity of a lifetime. In fact, I'm quite sure it's one for the history books." Nervous, he tried to make a joke, "I always wanted my own Wiki page."

Innes ignored the joke and continued, "Do you plan to have any children after the procedure?"

Anne met Genne's eyes, then responded, "We weren't planning to, but you never know. I mean, we both come from small families. Early in our marriage we chose to focus on our careers and enjoy life. Having kids at our stage of our life just doesn't make sense." She added, somewhat reflectively, "It's not something we completely dismissed, but we're both in our forties, so it's highly unlikely."

"That's completely understandable, Anne," Innes reassured her. She then placed a tablet in front of them and continued more formally, "Here are the terms of our agreement, if you wish to read them again."

Anne and Genne began reading intently, scrolling down with their fingers.

Innes explained, "In essence, you are agreeing to undergo genetic modification procedures where your current genes will be altered to provide a number of enhancements, as discussed and recommended by Mannix." She paused, making eye contact with both of them, then continued, "All treatments, recovery, and follow-up healthcare will be provided free of charge. In return, however, you give Mannix complete and unequivocal rights to publicize the procedure, it's results, and its impact for the next twenty years." She looked directly into their eyes again and continued, "This also means you are not allowed to release any information regarding the procedure without our explicit approval." She paused dramatically to ensure that they agreed unequivocally.

"This procedure is sure to attract a lot of attention from the media and various organizations. There will be a lot of pressure even from your family to disclose details of the procedure, but you must understand this work is highly classified. That's one of the reasons our facility is located on a military base. We will be placing similar conditions on various media agencies we work with. Revealing any information without our express approval will have severe legal and financial consequences. This technology would be extremely dangerous if it finds itself in the wrong hands."

Anne nodded and held Genne's hands as he continued reading the tablet, then reaffirmed, "We understand."

Innes continued further, "This will include numerous media appearances, research papers, and regular health screenings."

Anne followed up, worried. "Based on Friday's session, do you think we are at risk from crazy people who believe this procedure to be immoral?" She avoided recalling the shouts like "abomination" during the debate.

Innes looked at them and spoke softly but confidently, "Yes, there are certain groups that believe our work is unnatural, the same way some religious groups believe even a common blood transfusion is unnatural. We've been dealing with these groups for many years now. We purposefully release information about the procedure in pieces. We monitor opposition as we release more information to ensure your safety. We will assign a security detail to your house if necessary. If your life is ever in danger, we will move you to a secure location."

Genne asked, "How much do you think this will interfere with my work?"

Innes replied after a moment, "I don't think you understand how this will change your lives, both of your lives. At the beginning, you may decide to return to your old life. Quickly you will realize you are now a pioneer and the first proof of an era long awaited by scientists, writers, and futurists alike. You will become famous. To put it simply, there will be no need for either of you to work."

Genne grinned, "Wow. Celebrity life and no more daily grind," but Anne hesitated, unsure how this level of media attention would alter their life and marriage.

As Innes's last statement hung in the air, Mannix arrived via the same elevator. As he stepped out, all of the walls changed color to earthy red, and quiet, harmonious background music filled the area. A quote appeared and remained on the wall across from the elevator, "The greatest tribute to the past is to outgrow it," attributed to F. M. Esfandiari. The walls remained partly translucent as lights traveled through them, matching the rhythm of the music. They became vibrant and almost alive. He approached and greeted them. "Welcome. Today we make history. How did you enjoy your stay in Boston?"

Anne replied, "It was wonderful. Thank you very much for your generosity, Dr. Haldanne."

He waved it off. "Please don't mention it. And please, just call me Mannix. I hate formalities." Mannix walked around and sat on the opposite side of the S-shaped table. He placed a small, pebble-like item on the table. As he did that, Genne's personal information was projected into the air directly above them. Mannix spoke, reviewing the information. "I see Innes already went through all of the pre-screening questions."

After a moment of reviewing the documentation on his screen, he looked at them and smiled. "Do you have any other questions before we proceed?"

Anne hesitated, then spoke. "Yes, there was one question your gadget could not answer and we were too shy to ask before."

"Of course," Mannix encouraged. "Ask away."

Genne bit his lip before asking, "Is this procedure … reversible?"

Mannix grimaced as if insulted by the question, but quickly regained his composure and answered with confidence. "I've already performed similar genetic-modification procedures thousands of times, and I have not had a single person want to reverse its effects. If you're not sure about this, let's stop right now."

"No that's not what I mean," Genne spoke defensively. "Of course I want to proceed with this. I was just wondering."

Mannix leaned back, folded his hands, and said, "Genne, the procedure is technically reversible. In fact, one of your eyes will remain unchanged. It's quite an isolated organ, perfect for keeping your original genetic code for reference. However, this is a highly complex procedure. It's really taxing both physically and mentally. Reversing it can be dangerous."

Mannix leaned over forward and continued, "Genne, I'll be honest with you. If you have any doubts, I'll go with someone else. Doing this procedure and then reversing it two years from now would suggest it's not effective. Please treat this as a one-way trip." He added reassuringly, "I have no doubt you will never want to return to your original normal self."

Genne was apologetic and overcompensated. "Forget I asked that question. Let's proceed!"

Anne looked at Genne with concern. "Hon, you know I love you and will support your decision on this."

Genne glanced over at her. "I know dear," and touched her hand. Then he looked back at Mannix and said, with all of the confidence he could muster, "Let's do it!"

Mannix smiled. "That's the spirit!"

He then typed a few letters on a projected keyboard and a list of enhancements appeared. "Based on your genetic profile, I've created a modification sequence with the following enhancements. First, we'll remove your genetic predispositions for cancer, depression, thyroid disease, kidney disease, and diabetes. Second, we will increase your metabolism and testosterone production. That will increase your energy level and confidence and decrease body fat. Third, we will alter your brain cells to increase focus, memory, response, recall, and, ultimately, your IQ. Finally, we will alter your liver and other organs to improve your natural immunity, ability to deal with stress, and increase long-term health. That last one will, among many other things, increase your overall health and life span. How does that sound?"

Genne was almost speechless with disbelief. "… wonderful."

Mannix continued, "Post-procedure, you will remain in the facility for a few days. We'll be observing how your body adapts to changes. After that, we will send you home with a monitoring device. Familiar surroundings help with mental recovery. We will still check on you every day. After two months, you should be ready to start your new life. Of course, during that time we'll cover all living expenses so you can focus on recovery. Think of it as a vacation or health leave. No need to work. I imagine these enhancements will give you a new perspective on life." He paused before finishing, "Now, when do you want to start?"

Anne responded, "We talked about this already. Please give us two weeks to get our affairs in order, pack, and prepare. Since we need to keep the procedure confidential, we'll tell our family and friends we're leaving the country for a long-overdue vacation."

Mannix looked at Innes. "We have preparations on our side as well." He got up, walked over, embraced them both, and smiled "Innes will take over from here. I'll see you on the day of your procedure." He then looked at Genne and Anne with excitement and finished, "And again, congratulations on making history."

Chapter 7: A Prisoner

Glenn sat across from a young, British man. The interview room was much nicer than typical interrogation rooms. It had windows, comfortable chairs, wallpaper, and the doors weren't locked. Regardless, the young man was very nervous.

"Relax, I just want your help with something. There is no need for you to be alarmed," Glenn tried to sound reassuring.

"Just give me a minute. Last time I was at the police station, it didn't end well," said the man.

Glenn continued, "You said your name is Scott Connor. The head of the GPRP provided your name and records."

Scott replied, still uneasy, "That's right. Scott is my name. I was told to talk to you about the program."

Glenn said encouragingly, "I really appreciate your time. I just want to remind you that you are not in any trouble. I'm simply curious about the Genetic Prisoner Reform Program."

Scott shook his head. "Don't mind me. Ask away. Gotta leave soon. Work in one hour."

Glenn wasted no time. "So, why were you in the program? Life sentence without chance of parole?"

Scott looked insulted. "No way, man! Not one of those crazies looking for a second chance." He avoided eye contact. "Thief. Stole a car. Drunk driving. Hit and run DUI. Got eleven years."

"So why were you in the program?"

Scott replied, looking to the side, "Was sick. Really sick. Cancer. Stage three."

Glenn leaned forward, curious. "Cancer. That's a bitch. So Mannix forced you to be a lab rat?"

Scott looked up angrily. "No way! Mannix is a good man. He offered to help. Lots of guys wanted a way out of slammer. Different with me. Dying. Simple choice. Had to volunteer." He looked back down. "Rather be a lab rat than a dead rat."

Glenn backed down, "Okay. My bad. I didn't mean to push. Do you want any coffee or a cig?"

Scott replied, "Nope. Gotta go to work. Let's do it. Just get it over with."

Glenn decided he would probably get more information if he left the questions open. "Just tell me the whole story and you can go."

"Sure," Scott looked up again and began talking. "Got put into Ironwood. Hit and run DUI like I said. Blythe, California. Waiting for chance of parole after six. Four years in, one night I passed out, heavy coughing. Doc sent me for tests. Wham. Stage three. Fancy name melanoma. In my lungs." He paused, trying to regain control of his emotions. "First it got really bad. Was weak. Tried chemo. Didn't work shit." He looked away, ashamed. "Met bad people in the slammer. Got into nasty drugs. Wanted to forget. One night I OD'd. Almost didn't wake up." Tears appeared in his eyes. He wiped them quickly, looked away again, and continued, "Mannix came, asking for volunteers. Said he wanted to help. Said he can't change our pasts. But said he can change our futures. Said he could free us. Free us from prison, free us from ourselves, addiction, violence, sickness like cancer." Scott looked up for a moment again. "Had nothing to lose, man. Cancer was killing me. Drugs were killing me. The hole was killing me. I signed." He stopped abruptly.

Glenn asked gently, "What did you sign?"

Scott returned, "Didn't care. I signed. Anything else was better than slammer."

"You look thirsty. You sure you don't want some water?

"Sure. Water is good."

Glenn got up and poured a glass of cold water. "Keep going. I don't want you to be late for work."

Scott continued, "Mannix is a good man. Didn't just cure cancer. Changed me. Made my body better. Made me better. Two weeks waited. Truck came in. Took us to some kind of place. Put us to sleep. Did whatever. I don't remember nothing. Woke up two days after, fresh as rain."

Glenn asked, surprised, "You mean you don't remember anything about the procedure?"

Scott shrugged. "Like I said, nothing. They gave me a shot. I woke two days later."

"Do you understand how the procedure worked?"

Scott took a gulp of water and responded, "Some gene mixin' magic science. Dunno. Don't care. Just wanted to feel better."

"Okay, keep going," Glenn directed.

Scott continued, "Woke up fresh as rain. Felt so good. No cancer. No pain. No fear. Didn't crave booze. Didn't want drugs. Felt so free."

"That sounds wonderful. Good for you. Keep going …"

Scott looked up with joy on his face. "New life, bro. Felt strong. Got early parole. Mannix sent special doctors to monitor me and crap. Made me feel even better. Three months later, I got parole. Helped me find a job. I do breakfast in the hotel. Fry cook. Honest job. Even help. Volunteer at humane society. Love walking dogs. Gave me contacts."

Glenn interrupted, confused. "You mean contact lenses?"

Scott leaned forward and pointed to his eyes. "Yeah. Hetero-somethin'-or-other. One eye changed color. Other stayed the same."

Glenn whispered quietly, almost to himself, "Heterochromia."

Scott nodded. "Yeah, that's it," then pronounced it slowly, in syllables. "He-te-ro-chro-me-a. Contacts everyday. Else people stare. Think I'm a freak or somethin'." He took another sip of water.

"How long ago was that? How are you feeling now?" Glenn asked.

Scott replied, smiling, "Two years. Feeling good. Feeling strong. Top-of-the-world, baby! Beer and football on Saturdays. Even go on dates, oh yeah. Fresh as rain."

Glenn was not interested in those details, so he said, "That's great. Can you tell me anything more about Mannix or any of his associates? Anything suspicious?"

Scott raised his voice, almost outraged. "You don't get it! This man a saint! Freed my mind! Gave me hope. Gave me a new life. If you …"

Glenn interrupted, raising his hands, "Relax! I'm not investigating Mannix. I'm just asking a few questions about the program."

"Fine. But that man is a saint, you hear!?"

Glenn said "Okay. Okay. Saint. Got it. So who else was in the program with you?"

Scott shrugged his shoulders. "Dunno. Don't care. Maybe twenty other thugs. Some really sick. Some on life sentence. No parole. No hope. Really mean sons of bit..." He stopped himself.

"Any guys this procedure didn't go as planned?"

Scott thought for a minute. "Dunno. All the guys I was with were good. Great. Miracle. Like me."

"Do you know where any of them are right now?"

Scott shook his head. "No way. Dunno where they are. Strict orders. No contact. Not a whisper to anyone. Unless told. Like you. Was told to talk to Agent Abbot. Anything he asks."

Glenn knew he wasn't getting anywhere. "How about Innes? Can you tell me anything about Innes?"

"Inne-who? Don't know who that."

"You mean you never met Innes Tannah? She leads the Genetic Prisoner Reform Program."

Scott shook his head again. "Don't know any In-nes Tan-nah," he said, struggling to pronounce the name the best he could. "I would remember strange name like that. Never met her," he added.

Glenn asked, puzzled, "So who administered the treatment to you?"

Scott grimaced. "Dunno. Docs didn't use real names. Just strange name tags like DS, FT, SL, and crap. No real names."

Glenn was scratching his head. "Did you ever meet another prisoner named Lenny? Lenny Small?"

Scott grinned, repeating, "Funny name. Small." He paused, thinking, then replied, "Nope. Maybe another slammer. Met thugs from other places. Nobody named Small." He took another sip of water.

"Anything else you want to tell me about the program?"

Scott shook his head. "Real shame normal folks can't do it. Cancer is shit. Mannix could help others. He said feds won't let him. But one day. He said he is trying. One day he will."

Glenn rose from his chair. "Thank you for coming, Scott. Your information and perspective was very helpful." He reached out and shook the man's hand.

"Happy to help." Scott shook the agent's hand, took the last sip of his water, and placed the glass back on the table.

Agent Abbot escorted the visitor out of the room, dismissed him, then returned into the interview room. He put on a latex glove and took out a small plastic evidence bag. He carefully placed the glass Scott was drinking from in the bag and sealed it. He took off the latex glove and walked across the hallway to a door labeled Forensics, talking to himself *There is one more question, Mr. Connor, that you will answer for me…*

Chapter 8: The Procedure

Two weeks passed quickly. Anne and Genne Manning wrapped up all their preparations. A dark limo with two security guards picked them up from their home in California and escorted them to a small airport. From there, a small private plane flew them back to Boston where another limo and security detail were waiting.

The doors to the vehicle opened and Innes greeted them with a slight smile. "Welcome back. How are you doing?"

Genne responded while getting into the car, "Nervous and excited at the same time."

Anne added, "More nervous than excited," as she sat down.

Innes responded, "That's quite normal. I assure you there is nothing to worry about. I'll brief you during our travel to the facility. Everything in order?"

"Yes," Anne responded. "Our families think we're traveling to Greece. Genne took a short leave of absence from work…," then

47

rushed on. "No details provided, of course. Nothing posted on Facebook. Neighbors will water plants..."

Genne agreed, "I'm ready to change the world."

Innes smiled in response. "That's brilliant. Thank you for your discretion."

Genne cracked his neck and popped "Okay, hit me. What's next?"

Innes looked at the tablet in front of her and began explaining the agenda. "Right now, it's eleven o'clock Eastern. We will board a special transport at eleven thirty. It will take us to our secure facility. We should arrive there about one-thirty this afternoon. We'll give you thirty minutes to unpack and settle in your room. At two o'clock, Genne will undergo preliminary health assessment including blood pressure, blood tests, urine, stool, stress test, MRI, ECG, and so on. Both of you will also undergo psych evaluations. That will take us to six o'clock. We have a special meal prepared for Genne to ease his recovery." She paused to look up, checking for any questions, then got back to her list "At seven o'clock we will prep Genne for the procedure. He will be placed in a special medical pod, connected to various monitoring devices. We will monitor his vitals, ensuring he is stable. If all goes well, we'll administer a sedative at eight p.m. He will fall into a deep sleep until the procedure is over, approximately twenty-four hours later."

Innes looked at Anne. "I'm sorry, Anne, but the procedure is highly confidential. You will not be able to attend. We have a special room available for you. Various doctors and specialists will work with you to develop a personal recovery and support plan. We know this process will be emotionally taxing for you as well. This will keep your mind focused and productive. We don't want you to worry unnecessarily."

She then looked at Genne. "Genne, you will be semi-conscious and under constant monitoring for at least two days. You will be partly sedated during this time. Your body has to recover first. You will then be moved to a recovery centre where Anne can join you. Our focus will shift to your mental recovery and forming a new identity."

"What will his new identity be?" Anne asked.

Innes responded, looking back at Anne. "Don't worry, you will have your real husband back and unharmed. He will be the same man, just better." She paused, then said reassuringly, looking at both of them, "We have the very best doctors and psychiatrists on staff. There is nothing to worry about. You will be fine. We have done these procedures thousands of times."

"You will remain under observation in our facility for a few more days," she continued. "We will then take you home to recover further. You will remain under close monitoring with daily visits and tests. We will temporarily install a few cameras outside of your house for additional security."

Innes continued explaining and reassuring as they arrived in a large, white, windowless room filled with seats around a medium-sized oval table. They followed her directions and strapped themselves to the chairs. They sensed the room begin moving. Innes briefed them on various security procedures, facility maps, and key staff they would be meeting. Strangely, they used two- or three-letter acronyms instead of names for the staff. Innes also summarized post-recovery procedures, including meditation and other exercises for when they finally got home.

Time flew. They must have finally arrived at the facility, because the room stopped moving. The doors opened to a completely different environment. It resembled the intake area for a hospital emergency room. Various doctors and nurses were awaiting their arrival and attended to them immediately. Genne was asked to lie down on a hospital bed, while one of the nurses held Anne's hand. Staff guided them through an unusual tunnel. Its walls were cross-woven with alternating semi-translucent and wood-like material. The semi-translucent material pulsed with light traveling in the direction they were heading. All of the staff with them wore large glass bands covering their ears and eyes, all the way to the backs of their heads. Anne noticed various information was displayed on the peripheral areas of these strange glasses. She even noticed a talking face on one of the displays.

They entered a large, white, circular hall. All of the surfaces were made of the same material and displayed various information. A series of doors, approximately twenty, were spread evenly throughout the hall on both sides. Another hallway was opposite where they entered. Some of the doors had names and other details right beside them on the wall, including graphical representation of vital signs. Anne could not recognize other details. Patient names were not shown. Instead, two- or three-letter initials were displayed. Above them, the same white material became much brighter, illuminating the whole area.

Right in the middle of the hall, another central structure stood separated and guarded, secure from the visitors. Anne could only see some displays in the distance. Details were distorted from her angle, protected from curious eyes. Several attendants keenly reviewed the information shown. They, too, were wearing the glass head bands. They even seemed to be talking to each other without turning their heads. Their uniforms were also color coded. Two groups escorted them, wearing green and yellow uniforms. Inside the central structure, most people were wearing red uniforms. Guards wore blue. All of the colors had soft, earthy tones. Anne didn't recognize the fabric. It was nothing she had seen before, silky and flexible, yet strong.

Genne was wheeled into a room, Anne following. It was a well-lit area, the size of two large living rooms. As they entered, the outside noises faded rapidly as if somehow cancelled. Again, the walls, floor, and ceiling were connected and made of the same material. In the middle stood another strange-looking hospital bed. On the wall opposite the door was a massive display. The back featured a full-wall window and a small sitting area with a table, plus two elegant armchairs. Genne was moved to the bed while Anne approached the window. She was hoping to satisfy some of her curiosity about where they were. The window was a few floors above the base of the building. It looked like they were surrounded by rich, tropical vegetation. In the distance, she saw a small mountain range and a sandy coast. As she neared the window, she heard various forest noises such as wind and birds singing. For a moment she was captivated by the stunning view. When she looked down, she saw other parts of a building. It had a strange shape, tall and cylindrical like a tree, with short exit tunnels like roots. A single drop of water slid down the massive window. She touched it, tracing as it wandered down. As her fingers moved, the window became less translucent and tinted white. Once she realized what was happening, she traced her fingers back up and the beautiful view returned. She ran her finger across the window. The volume of sounds faded away. She smiled, wondering if this beautiful view was a projection and not real at all. She turned back to Genne and saw various medical staff attending him.

Gene had already changed into a hospital gown, primarily covering his front. One of the nurses, wearing yellow, was checking his pulse. Another one was placing special stickers, probably for the ECG. Yet another was adjusting an elastic cap with sensors inside it. The last one placed a watch-like monitoring device on his left wrist. Another person, wearing green, was supervising, checking things off on a tablet, and talking to Genne. Once everything was set up, the person in green—*The doctor?* Anne wondered—pressed some buttons and all of the vital signs appeared on the wall behind the patient, not visible to him.

The bed was like no other hospital bed Anne had ever seen. It must have had sensors, because it automatically adapted to the phases of the procedures. It lowered and folded into a chair when Genne first approached it. It straightened flat when nurses applied various sensors. It tilted when one of the doctors needed to speak to him. The bed was made of the same special material she noticed in the limo where they first met Mannix. It looked like a coral reef but was soft and flexible. It was very responsive to touch and pressure. It appeared to hold Genne gently, but securely. At one point, something that looked like a tentacle came from inside the bed and wrapped around his hand. It started to pulsate, as if delivering a liquid into his bloodstream.

A few moments later, Mannix appeared on the wall. His projection literally walked across the wall in Genne's room. He waved, somehow aware of their presence at the end of the room. "How are you, Genne? How are you, Anne? It's an exciting time. We're making history!"

Genne's drugs were kicking in fast. "Are you here, Mannix?"

"In a manner of speaking...," Mannix responded charmingly. "I could not attend in person, but I made sure there was time to speak to you before the procedure started."

"I want to thank you...," Genne's words became quite slurred, "... for taking me ... doing this ..." till he quickly faded and fell asleep.

Mannix grinned and turned his attention to Anne. "How are you, dear? Did all of the preparations go well?"

A number of new staff members entered the room, including two guards in blue uniforms. They were carrying a medium-sized, but heavy-looking, case. As they approached the bed, another arm grew out of the bed. The guards opened the case and removed a large cylindrical object, which they carefully placed on the new bed arm. Another doctor approached the container, pressed a few buttons on his tablet, and the arm retracted, swallowing the cylinder.

Anna asked, "What is that?"

Mannix grinned and responded, "That is the secret sauce... key piece of the technology that turns mere mortals into giants." He watched Genne, then added, "Anne, we will now be moving Genne to a pod where he will safely undergo the rest of the procedure." He looked straight into her eyes. "During this time, we'll help you prepare for what's ahead."

Anna raised her hands to her face, trying to contain waves of emotion, but tears were already falling. She whispered a soft "Okay."

Mannix reassured her softly. "Anne, I know this is difficult. Important things in life are often very difficult. I promise you that no harm will come to your husband." He continued as two nurses approached Anne and led her out of the room. "I'm sorry, but you cannot witness this part of the journey. It's really for your own benefit and protection."

Anne wasn't sure what he meant by that. Perhaps not knowing some of Mannix's secrets made her less of a target for the media, competitors, and crazies opposing Mannix's vision. She released another "Okay" as more tears fell. She paused and turned to exit the room. She waved to Genne and whimpered another "Okay, I'll see you soon dear … Wishing you sweet dreams… no nightmares."

Chapter 9: Room Full of Rabbits

Agent Abbot did not have a search warrant. In fact, he was about to break into the apartment of a man he speculated was responsible for a brutal murder a few days ago. He hoped that Mr. Lenny Small did, in fact, live in a quiet, inexpensive, fifteen-storey suburban apartment building. He was admiring the modern architecture and the location, bordering on a generous park and about a five-minute walk from a variety of amenities including a mall, groceries, and a subway line: Everything a loner like Mr. Small would want. While approaching, he wondered if a divorced FBI agent might also want to live there.

Glenn did not show his badge at the gate. In fact, he didn't want to be recognized, especially at this late hour. Security was sparse and outdated. He easily sneaked inside, following another tenant. A sluggish elevator took him to the eleventh floor, where he veered right to find apartment twenty-two.

He paused in front of the door, looked around, then listened intently. What if instead of a dead man's condo he was about to break into the home of a very much alive and likely angry ex-prisoner? A few versions of this scene ran through his head. One where he broke into a living room full of drug-dealers who penalized his interruption with unimaginable weaponry to repaint the hallway blood red. A version, where he walked in on a startled naked man just walking out of a shower, either screaming or, worse, extending an invitation. In yet another version, he simply got the apartment wrong and barged in on an elderly couple having a quiet dinner, perhaps startling someone and causing a heart attack. He wasn't sure what version he preferred.

Reassured by silence, he pulled out his lock picks and, with few twists, unlocked the door. He slowly and gently pushed the door forward, peering inside. He paused for a second before entering completely and locking the door behind him. He panned left then right, looking for any movement. He took a few steps forward and scanned inside the kitchen, then a small living room. The furniture was simple but tasteful, mostly cherry wood and dark leather. He moved slowly through the hallway with a flashlight in his hand. He peeked into the first room, a large bedroom. He then veered left to check the bathroom. He ended his exploration with a smaller bedroom in the most distant part of the apartment. He cracked the door as quietly as he could. He walked inside and stopped, stunned.

This was a library. Unlike the other sparse rooms in this apartment, this room was furnished with bookcases on all sides. In the middle was a comfy armchair with a side table and a small lamp. The window had sheer curtains, allowing lots of light inside during daytime. Only one picture frame, hung directly above the light switch. Three people posed in a gentle embrace facing the camera: A tall skinny middle-aged man stood between Innes and Mannix. Glenn recognized the murderer from his investigation, Lenny Small. He was relieved that his instincts once again proved to be correct.

Glenn spent a few minutes examining the room. Custom-made floor-to-ceiling cherry wood bookcases were filled with printed paperback travel books and magazines highlighting different tourist attractions. Stickers on the shelves listed different cities around the world: Cairo, Hong Kong, London, Mexico City, Rome, Moscow, Amsterdam, Paris, Baghdad, Manila, Toronto, Monaco, Lima, Beijing, Dublin, Jakarta, Tokyo, and so many more. Travel guides, sightseeing photo panoramas, quick translators, restaurant guides, geography books, travel magazines, and even promotional flyers… everything meticulously categorized and organized. The central armchair was well worn. Although clean at the moment, the wooden coffee table revealed some wear-and-tear as well as coffee stains.

Glenn continued to examine the shelves, hoping to find a section with classics or fiction. He explored meticulously catalogued and organized libraries. He found nothing but travel. He checked again in disbelief. Every single book in this home library excited the reader with visions of travel to unique destinations and promises of once-in-a-lifetime experiences. *So many rabbits…* he thought. *Poor man, his dreams were never realized.*

Frustrated, he searched the rest of the house but found nothing of importance. He checked the garbage, cupboards, and even the pantry. Still nothing. In fact, the home looked too clean. His instincts told him he would not find what he was looking for here. More likely the apartment was searched and staged by H+ immediately after the murder was discovered. He went back to the bathroom. He checked the cabinet for any medication or illegal substances. Again, he found nothing. He turned around and looked at the mirror. He noticed some spots on the bottom part of the mirror, no doubt from brushing teeth or shaving. He looked at closer and saw slight distortions in the surface. His instincts took over. He turned the hot water on full and waited as steam rose slowly, caressing the mirror. He closed the bathroom door and kept waiting. Within a few minutes, letters appeared on the glass surface. He half-suspected what the message would be. That didn't make him less concerned. In fact, he very much regretted what he saw. He turned off the water and read it to himself *big brother is watching you*. The letters were written by a finger, no doubt Lenny's. *He knew he was being watched, and this was the only way he can provide another clue*. Glenn took out his com device and took a picture.

He now realized why Lenny longed to travel, yet never did. He was constantly monitored and controlled by these people. This prison reform program simply exchanged physical prison cells for monitoring devices worn on the wrist. He was never allowed to leave the watchful eyes of the GPRP. His dreams colliding with such reality would have been unbearable.

Glenn snapped back out of his thoughts and knew not to wait any longer. He returned to the library and pocketed the picture frame. He followed his instincts, backtracked through the hallways, and took the stairs instead of the elevator. He suspected Mannix had planted numerous monitoring devices, including cameras, in the home. He cursed himself for not being more careful and sweeping it before entering. The place looked too clean in the first place. He wondered if Lenny used the nickname George to refer to either Mannix or Innes. He wondered if there was something more to the relationship between Innes and Lenny. Perhaps that's why Innes had treated Glenn so harshly. She may have simply been trying to hide her emotions. Perhaps they knew each other prior to the procedure. Perhaps they were involved romantically. Perhaps Lenny wasn't dreaming of traveling alone.

Glenn exited the building through a side entrance. He intentionally made eye contact with the security camera. He wanted Mannix and Innes to know he was not afraid. He wanted them to know he was finally able to confirm Lenny's identity. He wanted them to know he was committed to finding out the truth, no matter the cost. Then he disappeared into the night.

Chapter 10: Crisis of Faith

"What do you believe?" asked a woman, roughly in her late fifties, sitting across from Anne. Her uniform was pink, unlike any of the others. Her name tag read JHJ. They sat in comfortable armchairs, looking at another beautiful view.

"What do you mean?" Anne responded, confused.

The woman continued, "You are about to go through a dramatic life change. What you believe will shape how you understand this experience and how you adapt to it. I'm here to help you through this journey. So," she paused to emphasize the question. "What do you believe?"

Anne needed a moment to process this question. Her beliefs were quite personal, and she wasn't sure she wanted to share them with someone she had just met. "I'm sorry, I wasn't expecting this. It's quite an emotional time for me, for both of us." She rose, hesitated, then got an idea. "Would you mind telling me first what you believe? It would help me open up."

JHJ smiled in understanding. "I don't mind at all dear." She leaned back and started "I believe the society must progress from religion to science to evolve. It's the same renaissance that gave birth to art and medicine in the fifteenth and the sixteenth centuries. And I believe genetic modification provides human species with enormous potential to evolve past their wildest expectations, and in this very generation. I am here precisely to help that cause. My grandfather called this *secular humanism*." The woman in the pink uniform now leaned forward, ready to write notes on her tablet. "How about you, Anne?"

"That sounds so simple," Anne began. "I wish I was as clear and convicted about my beliefs." She began to pace a little, walking back and forth while looking through the window wall. She kept looking into the distance, keeping her emotions at the base as she explained. "Some things are easy. I do believe in science. How could I not? I'm here." She paused, biting her nails. "Science is how we understand the world around us. It explains what was once unknown. We use it to improve this world including ourselves. We use it to heal sicknesses." She hesitated, "but also to create them." She looked at JHJ, finally able to articulate the essence of her thought. "I think science is also a creative expression of who we are. We want to believe it's impartial, but it's not. How could it be? We ourselves are biased. We twist it to suit our needs."

JHJ interrupted, "But science is based on fact."

Anne smiled. "Yes, but our minds aren't. It's both a curse and a blessing of being human. Let me explain." She sat down to continue. "We want to believe in a world ruled by logic, not emotion. A world explained and controlled purely by science and not God. Which one requires more faith? Which one grapples harder with our insecurity, grasping to control the unknown?" She raised her hands, wide apart. "I live in a duality. On one side and in this very moment I can see the wondrous power of what science can do. And I am profoundly amazed. On the other side, I cannot deny the evidence of natural harmony in this world. All evidence shows this world was intentionally and intelligently designed. And that both humbles me and scares me." She reunited and dropped her hands. "I always thought that the only way to truly understand and experience this world... was to truly consider all the options."

"You mean science cannot be impartial and requires faith same as divine creation," JHJ clarified.

"Yes." Anne rose once again and paced as JHJ listened intently. "I don't think science is a destination. It's a method of traveling. Depending on your belief and values, it is a way of either understanding the creator or becoming the creator."

"So which side do you believe in?"

Anne looked at the beautiful nature scene through the window, wondering if it was manufactured or real, and answered, "I'm not sure I've decided yet." She paused caught in her thoughts then concluded, "Probably a bit of both."

"Tell me more..."

"I am very insecure. I see all of my imperfections all of the time. I want to change them. I want to become better. And science is so wondrous at understanding the human body, psychology, nature..." she paused before continuing. "But there is so much we still don't understand. There are scientific theories we disprove as we reach new levels of understanding. I think... Maybe we want science to be the answer because it's something we understand and control, but really we're just as scared as the people who trust in God regardless of the facts in front of them."

JHJ posed another question. "Do you believe in evolution?"

Anne glanced at her and answered matter-of-factly, her hands moving "Sure. We are all evolving on many levels even throughout our own life. We learn and grow. We love."

JHJ shook her head, clearly expecting a different answer, but Anne interrupted. "Dr. Bell had an interesting theory about evolution..."

JHJ was caught mid-thought but nodded encouragingly.

Anne again sat down. Her hands were now animated, as if she was painting a canvas in midair while talking. She was visibly excited, like a kid doing show-and-tell. She started, "In his book *True Human Evolution*, he argued that evolution of the mind must come before evolution of the body. That we must first evolve away from selfishness, pride, and violence before our bodies can evolve. How can we create perfection without truly knowing what it is?"

JHJ's brow furrowed. "Not sure we need to wait. We already know we want to live forever. We want to acquire more knowledge. We want to overcome our physical and mental limitations—"

Anne interrupted again. "What is your favorite painting?"

JHJ struggled to answer, even more confused now. "I'm not sure how this is relevant…"

"I like Picasso for his unique creativity and Van Gogh for capturing so much emotion."

"Sorry, but how is this connected to our current conversation?"

"These paintings are highly regarded as some of the most beautiful in human history, yet by many standards they are far from perfect."

JHJ tilted her head, brow still furrowed. "How so?"

Anne's hands raised and gestured, "Because they are an inaccurate representation of nature and life as perceived through our eyes … through science."

JHJ twitched, trying to remain calm but growing impatient. "I see art as a form of personal expression. However, what I am trying to understand here is what you understand and believe about the very change your husband is going through at this very moment."

Anne bit her lip. "See, I think only perfection can birth perfection. We are imperfect, and by our very nature we can only birth imperfection." Her voice rose in excitement "We cannot make ourselves be gods. We have no clue what that even means." She continued, seeing JHJ's irritation, "Yet what we create has so much beauty, so much passion, so much wisdom. We seek to create something greater than ourselves precisely because we realize our frailty of life … and poverty of spirit … and the limitations of our wisdom…"

JHJ gave up, realizing the state Anne was in. "Perhaps this is enough for today." She rose and forced a smile, "I shall see you again tomorrow to continue our conversation."

Anne sensed her uneasiness. "I'm sorry if I've offended you in any way."

JHJ was caught off guard. "No, you didn't. Not at all, Anne. She smiled. "Why don't you rest, and I'll see you tomorrow."

Anne nodded and waved as JHJ closed the door behind her. Left to her own thoughts, she considered. The last few weeks and today had made her question everything she believed. Yet she embraced this struggle. She was invigorated by it. She knew this conflict would only result in a deeper understanding of herself. She reflected on Genne and longed to see him. She worried about the procedure. She worried about life going forward. She felt inadequate to handle whatever was ahead, but she knew she had the passion to break through it. She had faith she would land on her feet on the other side.

Chapter 11: Secrets

Innes watched Anne's session with JHJ, then checked her monitors for Genne's progress. He had just been placed in the pod where the genetic modification would take place over next few hours. It was time to update Mannix.

Her field office was extremely sparse. A square office with no furniture, just a sitting mat. The walls were covered with projections of information and video feeds. Above her, the ceiling was illuminated with a soft, yellow glow.

She motioned to dim the wall screens and knelt to refocus her mind in preparation for the connection. She was motionless for a few minutes, meditating and settling her mind. She tethered her feelings and rehearsed her key points. She took out her brown contact lenses and placed them in a small box in her pocket. Her eyes were two different colors, one light brown, almost red, the other light gray, almost white. The contrast was startling. In her mind, it was a constant reminder of her own personal change.

She saw Mannix as far more than a boss. The respect and admiration she had for him far surpassed any professional relationship. He was her sensei, her life mentor, her—

The silence was interrupted by a small flickering light. She motioned again and the room brightened. Mannix appeared on one of the walls. Innes did a formal forty-five percent *saikeirei* bow and greeted him in Japanese. "Ohayou gozaimasu Mannix sensei."

"Innes, please, these formalities are really not necessary. You are no longer the lost girl I found a few years ago. You matured and flowered into someone much greater than either of us could imagine."

Innes bowed again.

Mannix continued, "Please report. How are our guests?"

Innes responded, "Genne's procedure is on track. He finished stage one, preparation. He was just placed in the pod and started stage two, suspension. The remaining stages of modification, reanimation, reprogramming, and rehabilitation will proceed as scheduled."

"How about Anne? Am I sensing some concern?"

"Anne just finished her session with JHJ. It went as well as expected. I am waiting for the doctor's full report. I do believe that JHJ has a few concerns and recommended actions."

Mannix grinned. "JHJ always has concerns and recommendations. That's exactly why we hired her. She can identify and prevent potential problems well ahead of time."

Mannix's eyes narrowed. "Innes, Is there something else? I can see your heart monitors rising."

Innes nodded quickly. "Yes. The FBI is investigating the murder by Lenny Small."

Mannix thought for a minute. "That's strange. Wasn't he one of our GPRP success stories? Were you able to confirm what actually happened?"

Innes glanced away. "Circumstances are quite unusual. We do suspect foul play. Perhaps someone trying to undermine our program. I will continue using our contacts to understand what exactly transpired there."

"I'm not sure that's necessary, Innes. We could simply make it all disappear."

Innes waited, bowed slightly, and said, "That will not be necessary, Mannix sensei." She met his eyes while remaining slightly bowed. "Perhaps Agent Abbot can be of some use to us."

"Go on," Mannix said, intrigued.

Innes grinned ever so slightly and rose to her feet. "This may be deliberate sabotage to undermine events about to unfold. There are many people who do not yet appreciate your vision, Mannix sensei. Agent Abbot is proving to be quite resourceful. He may lead us to answers without our involvement." She paused to meet his eyes again. "We are monitoring his progress and restricting access to any H+ information."

Mannix nodded slowly. "Wise counsel, kohai. Proceed with caution."

"Arigatou gozaimasu. We will use strict discretion and keep an eye on the media as well." She bowed again.

"Oh, one more thing. Would you mind reminding JHJ to send me the latest results from yesterday's generic experiments? I want to review the report before it's sent to General Anders."

"Of course. I will find her immediately after this session."

Mannix raised his hand. "Thank you. I'll see you tomorrow."

Innes bowed again. "Sayonara, Mannix sensei."

As Mannix disappeared from the wall, Innes returned to her meditation to regain focus. She was still for sixty seconds, then rose suddenly and left her room whispering, "I hope you do not disappoint me, Agent Abbot."

Chapter 12: Visiting Dr. Bell

Agent Abbot walked into a small office at Harvard University. One side was filled with books. On the other side, four different computers and screens cluttered a large table. An old man rose from a well-seasoned rocker.

Glenn raised his hand to stop him. "Don't get up, Dr. Bell. Stay where you are." He sat beside the professor in a spare office chair and continued, "Thank you for meeting me on such short notice. I just have a few questions."

Bell looked at him closely. "Aren't you the young man from Friday? You called out how many chromosomes are in the human genome. Are you also a scientist?"

Glenn responded by showing his FBI credentials. "Nope, just an agent. But I know a thing or two about genetics. I even read some of your books. They were very insightful and surprisingly accessible."

Bell raised an eyebrow. "Don't flatter me, Agent Abbot. I'm far too old and grey for that." He added, grinning, "Unless you're one of my students trying to negotiate access to grant money."

Glenn grinned as well. "Definitely not here for your grant money, sir."

Bell met Glenn's eyes. "I dare speculate you are here to ask me about Mannix."

Glenn glanced away, looking for the best way to position his question. "Not exactly…"

Bell didn't wait for the rest. "I'm afraid, my dear young man, there is not much I can tell you about my charismatic protégé nor about the genetic technology he is about to unleash onto this fragile world."

"Wait, did you say he was your protégé? When?"

Bell leaned back in his chair to reminisce. "That's correct. Mannix was one of my students at Oxford."

"Please tell me what he was like as a student."

"Brilliant mind. Extremely driven. Fearless. Charismatic. Possibly the best student I've ever had." Bell stopped abruptly.

Glenn probed, "I get the feeling there's a 'but' coming..."

Bell tried to hide his sadness. "Mannix has always been haunted by his past."

"How so?"

Bell continued, hesitating. "Mannix was abandoned by his mother at the age of three. He spent most of his life in foster homes."

"What about the father?"

Bell replied, "Mannix didn't know who his father was till his early twenties. By then his father was already dead...," he ended awkwardly.

"What do you mean 'of sorts'? Is his father dead or not?"

"Technically speaking, his father was vitrified..." Seeing confusion on Glenn's face he explained, "He placed himself in cryonic suspension after facing death from pancreatic cancer." A moment of sad silence followed, then Bell continued, "Mannix is trying to fulfill his father's greatest vision and dream."

Interesting. And what would that be?"

"Total transformation and evolution of human life. Ultimately, an end to death through science and technology," Bell responded.

Glenn raised his eyebrows. "That's a challenge of a lifetime. Does he actually think he can do this?"

Bell glanced through his office window. "I'm not sure, Agent Abbot, but if anyone can, it's probably him. But I'm sure you didn't come to see an old man about something you can read in your agency files. I'm sure you are here for a different reason."

"Yes, of course. I'm investigating a murder committed by someone who underwent Mannix's genetic-alteration procedure not too long ago."

Bell's eyes opened wide. "Oh my. Are you certain, dear boy?"

"I cannot share details of the case. However, I was wondering if you would be able to provide a professional opinion on this matter," Glenn continued.

Bell's eyes lit up. "I understand." One hand cupped his chin, "Do go on."

"Hypothetically speaking, if such a procedure were possible, would it be safe?"

Bell shook his head. "Mannix is a man of conviction, but he is not reckless. He values life. If he was to practice his genetic science on the populace, he would have believed it was safe to the patient."

"So you do think the procedure is safe?"

"No, my dear boy. I said Mannix believes his procedure is safe. He would have to be convinced his science would not harm the patient. But that does not mean the actual procedure is safe."

"I'm not sure I understand."

"I am certain that Mannix's methods and science are sound and safe to the body," Bell explained. "However, we are much more than our genes. Our minds are complex. Our life history creates deep brain paths that cannot be altered through gene alteration." He grinned and continued, "It is easy to genetically alter an apple with no self-awareness, no passions, no fears. Changing a human being is altogether different. It's far more than genetics."

Glenn took a moment to absorb Bell's point. "So you do believe this procedure to be flawed and potentially dangerous?"

Bell sighed, then spoke carefully, considering. "Potentially." Then added quickly, "Depending on the stability of the patient's mind."

"Hypothetically, then, how would that manifest?"

Bell grinned. "I haven't the foggiest, dear boy. You may as well ask me what Holy Mary looks like. This territory is completely unexplored and unknown. Except, perhaps, by Mannix of course."

Glenn pushed, hoping for more. "Would such a person be capable of murder?"

Bell thought for a moment. "Possibly. Especially if their life had a violent past and they somehow regressed or reverted from their genetic alteration." He rushed to add, "But I have no idea how any of this could happen. In fact, I have no data to even form a hypothesis."

But Glenn was focused on something. "Wait, how could the genetic alteration revert or regress?"

Bell shrugged. "That all depends on how it was accomplished in the first place. Perhaps it was not successful in the first place and the genes reverted over time. Perhaps this evolved human was not able to cope with the stress of his past and reached some type of compelling event."

"Compelling event?"

"Yes, a specific event that caused a dramatic change in direction."

"Such as …?"

Bell shrugged. "A great many things … could be a past traumatic memory."

Glenn nodded. "Makes sense. What else?"

"I suppose it could be another genetic alteration agent."

"What do you mean?"

"Well, imagine a specific genetic alteration agent was used to complete the procedure. Then another agent was introduced at a later time to either revert or disrupt the original alteration."

Glenn's instincts were piqued. "What could this agent be?"

"Again, I really haven't got the foggiest, my boy, but it could be another agent similar to the one responsible for the original genetic alteration."

"How could I determine what it was?"

Bell shrugged again. "My boy, we are getting nowhere fast. I have spent my life trying to discover such an agent in the first place." Then he grinned, "I'll let you know if I discover one. Till then your guess is as good as mine."

"Can you tell me anything about Innes Tannah?"

Bell laughed, as if foreseeing future questions. "She is an enigma, dear boy. I've met her a few times. She is beautiful and fearless. Mannix personally chose her as his protégé, but we know very little who she is or where she came from." He continued, smiling, "I'm afraid she is your mystery to solve."

Glenn nodded, then asked, "Do you have any idea why Mannix's facility would be located on a U.S. Naval base?"

Bell's eyes met Glenn's sharply, his voice dropped ed and became very controlled. "Agent Abbot, there are hundreds of reasons why the U.S. military would be interested in genetic alteration technology, none of which I wish to entertain." He rose. "I'm afraid our session is over. I have important academic matters to attend to."

Glenn had expected this and didn't want to burn any bridges. "Of course, Dr. Bell. I am sorry to have taken so much of your time." He got up and slowly headed back to the office door.

Bell reached out to shake hands and offered, "I wish you fortune on your journey ahead, Agent Abbot." Then he added more reluctantly as their eyes met. "I pray to dear God that Mannix has not lost his post-humanist beliefs. Else we all have much to fear in the days ahead."

Chapter 13: A New Day

"Genne, how are you feeling?" JHJ repeated multiple times. His awareness was returning slowly.

He strained to open his eyes and finally saw JHJ talking to another nurse. That nurse pressed something on her tablet.

"We are decreasing our sedative. Let us know if you feel any pain." JHJ spoke slowly and clearly. She made eye contact and asked, "Do you recognize me?"

Genne finally muttered, "You're a doctor at Mannix's centre."

"Very good. Now, do you know my name?"

Genne responded slowly, "I don't know your name. Initials … JHJ."

She smiled. "Very good, you're becoming aware." She stopped leaning toward him and asked, "What is the last thing you remember?"

Genne broke eye contact, thinking, "Falling asleep in a crazy hospital bed getting ready for the procedure"

"Can you tell me who you are?"

Genne raised himself in the bed and started slowly. "My name is Genne Manning. I'm married to Anne Manning. I'm a marketing manager." He spoke more quickly as memories surfaced. "I love to ski and travel and try new foods—"

JHJ interrupted. "Good I think we're ready." She pressed something on her tablet, then continued, "Genne, we kept you sedated for twenty-four hours after the procedure. We wanted your brain to get used to the changes in your body before we brought you back to consciousness. Otherwise you would feel overwhelmed and confused. We'll take you through some tests, including cognitive-assessment exercises. Don't be surprised if you're able to perform much better than you are used to doing."

Genne nodded. "Sure. Let's do it."

JHJ smiled again. "Great. I will be mixing direct questions with memory tests and some exercises. Just answer whatever comes to your mind. Don't over think it."

Genne nodded.

She started "Okay, question number one: What is the capital of Italy?"

Genne responded, "Rome, pronounced 'Roma' in Italian."

She pressed a button on her tablet, then turned it back to him, showing the number eighty-nine. "What is this number?"

"Eighty-nine... also the eleventh number in the Fibonacci sequence."

JHJ turned the tablet back, pressed something, and continued, "Tell me an animal name that starts with the letter *X*."

Genne surprised even himself by recalling several. "Xanthus, xenarthra, xenops, and xerus."

"Excellent." She pressed another button and turned the tablet to him again. "What color is this?"

"Red, my favourite color."

She smiled. "Yes, it is," then pressed another button on her tablet and continued, "What is the square root of 15129?"

Genne responded, "123" to his own surprise.

She pressed another button. "Very good," paused to look at Genne's vital signs on the wall right behind him, then continued. "Let's do some word association. I'll say one word and you have to tell me the first word that comes to your mind." Genne nodded and she immediately said "Wine."

"Grape."

"Bag"

"Purse."

"Sick."

"Kids."

"Great response rate. Let's continue with regular testing." She pressed another button on her tablet "What is the height of the tallest mountain in Africa?"

"Mount Kilimanjaro, approximately 5,895 meters above sea level. That's 19,341 feet."

She pressed another button on the tablet and turned it to him, showing another color.

"Orange." He was getting a rush from being able to answer so quickly.

JHJ continued, "What was the name of the fourth U.S. president?"

Genne grinned "James Madison. March 4, 1809 to March 4, 1817. And the last one to wear the funny white wigs."

"Interesting observation." Then JHJ pressed a button and showed him yet another color on her tablet.

"Yellow. Color of the sun. Radius of 696 thousand kilometres, temperature 5,778 Kelvin."

She looked at the wall behind him, checked with the nurse nearby, who responded "Vitals stable and strong," then looked back at Genne and said, "We're almost done."

Genne teased, "Why, am I beating your score?"

She smirked. "Dear boy, you are beating everyone's score." She looked back to her tablet and proceeded, "I'm going to show you a geometrical shape. You will have to give me the volume of the object based on other data provided on the image." She turned the tablet back to Genne.

Genne squinted, thinking, then responded after a split second, "147 litres."

JHJ pressed another button on her tablet to reveal two more colors.

He knew the drill by now. "Green and blue."

Now she asked something unexpected. "Recall and multiply all of the numbers you've used as answers in the last few minutes. What do you get?"

He thought for a moment, then answered, "89, 123, 5,895, and 147... that's 9,486,287,055."

The nurse nearby was shaking her head in amazement.

JHJ smiled. "Last question for this test, Mr. Amazing. What are the next two colors in the sequence I showed you?"

"I believe we're listing the colors of the rainbow. The remaining colors would be indigo and violet."

JHJ put away her tablet, sat down on a nearby stool, and began, "Genne, if you don't mind we'll do something very different now. I want you to talk about yourself in third person. Refer yourself as GM, based on your initials." She met his eyes, checking to see if he followed her, then continued "And answer the question 'What does GM think is real?' Take as much time as you like."

"What is real? Hmm ... That's harder to explain." He inhaled deeply, looked into the distance, and began explaining. "GM's concept of reality is based on the cumulative experience of his life, both conscious and subconscious, both physically experienced as well as interpreted ... stored in his brain as memories, ideas, and feelings ... and evolved over time by synthesizing and simplifying into a type of general understanding people commonly refer to as a worldview. This worldview filters and tints all new experiences." He met her eyes again and summarized, "GM, just like everyone else, believes reality to be a reflection of his life's experiences."

"Thank you. So what would significantly change GM's worldview or belief system?"

Genne answered promptly, "Someone's worldview can be altered by profoundly life-altering experiences."

"And what happens if such an event would occur?"

He responded, "The filter adjusts to comprehend and accommodate the new reality found in that experience."

"How would that worldview compare to that of a six-year-old child?"

He grinned. "A child's filter is barely formed due to lack of data, and is therefore more accepting of change. The child would interpret and store that experience differently."

JHJ met his eyes sharply. "Please listen to me very carefully. Your concept of reality no longer reflects who you really are now. The cognitive test should have demonstrated that quite clearly. For example, your approximate IQ right now is 216." She paused, allowing her words to sink in. "Do not adapt your filter. It will not work. In fact, it will cause much pain and frustration." She used her index finger to touch Genne's forehead. "Be as a child. Create a new worldview from scratch based on your experiences from here forward." She removed her finger and continued, "Consider yourself born again with a new reality and a new worldview. Root yourself in this new beginning. Question your limits and embrace your every change.

"This is your new reality: You are now nothing short of super-human. Embrace your new existence. Don't question it. Evolve into all that you can be!"

Chapter 14: Research

Glenn was getting frustrated. His clearance was too low to access most of the information about Mannix, Innes, and Lenny Small. He had already gone to his boss to get higher clearance and been denied. "It's like playing hide and seek with a bag over my head. Even if I can find someone, they can kick me in the ass and run the other way," he groaned, burying his face in his hands. "And in the meantime, I'll keep stumbling and falling."

He had tried several international databases with no luck, as well as multiple government databases, birth registries, even income tax returns. "This is ridiculous. How the hell do I get this blindfold off?"

He wasn't sure how to stay ahead of the case, Mannix, and Innes. He had had a lingering thought since he met her. His instinct told him she somehow didn't fit. He needed more information about her.

He decided to take a walk and get some food. He stopped at a nearby coffee shop to get an egg salad sandwich and one more cup of bad, bitter-tasting coffee. While standing in line, his eyes were drawn to a screen. Annoyed, he whispered, "As if watching commercials while standing in line to pay for crappy coffee was not enough punishment." The ad was for an Internet service to discover your family tree and ancestry based on facial recognition, DNA samples, and personal information. He ignored it, paid for the coffee and sandwich, and went back to the office, grumbling, "What makes you think I actually want to know my crazy family?" He took out his com device, checked the time, then pocketed it.

Since regular methods lead nowhere, how about we try something different? He took out his com device again and decided to reach out to an old informant. He sent an encrypted message to a once-convicted, now mostly harmless but well-connected hacker nicknamed Blue. The message read, "Need a personal favor. Find out anything you can about Innes Tannah Dr Mannix right hand."

Blue responded within seconds, "Gonna cost you bro"

Glenn replied, walking back to the office, "What? Grandma's BBQ pulled pork sandwich?"

Blue replied, "20 large"

Glenn groaned and sent back, "Why so much"

Blue took a few moments to reply, "Too hot. Gotta go to China black market!"

Glenn was surprised but he trusted his contact. "10 grand plus Grandma's BBQ pulled pork sandwich?"

Blue replied, "You don't have no grandma. 20 large. You get what you pay for :)"

Blue added, "Need 24 hrs"

Glenn replied, "Deal," then thought, *You better not be hiring a hundred teens in China to hack into her Facebook page.* Then amended, *I take that back. She probably doesn't have a Facebook page. Not the type. Too many secrets.*

Glenn reached the office, parked his butt on a worn-out office chair, unwrapped the egg salad sandwich in all its smelly glory, placed his extra-large coffee on an old, well-stained 'Orlando,

Florida' coaster, and grunted, stretching his hands high. *That's as much yoga as I'm going to get this month.*

He thought about the case and Lenny. Not much to follow. A picture with Mannix and a bathroom quote. He decided to research Lenny's criminal past, but found nothing of relevance to this case. He tried to access prison files and anything related to the Genetic Prisoner Reform Program, but was denied access once more.

He took another bite of his sandwich, took a sip of coffee, and an idea popped into his head *I don't have access to any other source of info.*" He searched for Lenny on the Internet and found a blog. He devoured the content but found only posts about travel destinations. *"Strange, the last post was a month ago,* he noticed. *"He desperately wanted to travel but it looks like he never did.*

Is there anything that can point me to George? he thought

Just then, Jack walked in, a digital book in his hand. "That's great, Jack. You've finally decided to learn how to read," Glenn snickered.

Jack responded with a grin, "Somebody has to. You refused and are still watching cartoons."

Glenn continued, "This wouldn't be one of those naughty books about communism, would it?"

Jack laughed. "Nope. Harry Potter. My kids are reading it. Way more interesting than all the files I get to read in this hellhole."

"Yeah, I hear you. I've got a case right now. Avid reader murdered and remodeled victim's apartment with blood and organs…"

"Nice…"

Glenn continued, "… but I got no motive and nothing to go on. His apartment is full of books, but clean as a whistle."

Jack thought for a second, then suggested, "How about his library card?"

"Library card?" Glenn echoed.

Jack grinned. "Again, some fancy book connoisseurs sometimes go to this building called a library…" He grimaced at Glenn, teasing him. "If he was an avid reader, he would be going to the library. Large selection of content accessible for free."

Glenn grabbed his jacked, stopped himself, put his jacked down, and forced the rest of his sandwich into his mouth, then picked up his jacket up again and rushed toward the door, mumbling, "That's brilliant Jack. Thanks for the idea."

"While you're there, maybe a good idea to get yourself a library card so you can learn how to read!" Jack called after him.

Glenn waved to him awkwardly and ran toward his car. He was trying to figure out which library was the closest to Lenny's home and workplace.

Just then, a call interrupted his train of thought, "This is Anya from forensics. We ran the DNA test you requested on that glass. Very healthy DNA structure. Nothing special except for a rare abnormality."

"What kind of abnormality?"

The voice on the other end responded, "A type of marker somehow encoded into the DNA. A very specific protein sequence. Not natural."

Glenn interrupted, confused, "What's the sequence?"

The voice replied, "Uhmm. We're not sure how to read it. It could be binary: 01001000 00100000."

Glenn was puzzled "Binary?"

Anya explained "Yes, 01001000 00100000 stands for H+ in binary.

Nothing else makes sense."

Glenn was silent, trying to process it.

The voice continued, "Will there be anything else?"

Glenn responded slowly, still in thought. "No … Yes!" Could you check the DNA database to see if the murderer from case 1007009 carried the same marker?"

"Yes, we can. Off the books again?"

"Yes. Good reason. We suspect an insider deep in the agency may be involved."

She replied, rushing, "I get it. Anything else?"

"Also, can you check DNA databases for any other people with the same marker?"

The voice took a moment to reply. "That would take a very long time. It's not a common DNA structure. I would have to run a custom search."

"Start by focusing on anyone in federal prison in the last ten years."

"Okay, will do. I may need a day or two to get you these results."

"Thank you, Anya. Carry on." Glenn hung up and thought, *Only one person would have the audacity to put his signature on a human DNA strand ... Mannix.*

Chapter 15: Testing Limits

"We're going to play virtual squash," JHJ told Genne with great satisfaction.

Genne grimaced, "Virtual squash?"

"That's right, Mr. Manning. That racket you're holding has a number of sensors that relate its movement to the cube-shaped room you are in. You're wearing a wrist monitor and a number of sensors on your body to monitor your heart rate, pulse, blood flow, response rate, and many other things. We will be virtually displaying your opponent and controlling where the ball is going. I'm assuming you've played squash before and are familiar with its rules."

Genne grinned, "Yes, I played squash in college. I have to get the ball before it hits the ground the second time. I can bounce the ball off all of the walls as marked—"

JHJ interrupted, "That's good enough. Let's proceed." She executed a sequence of touches on her tablet and a hologram of a faceless opponent appeared in the room. Glass walls tinted slightly, showing areas he was allowed to use when playing. She added, "I warn you, as the game progresses, the ball will travel at extremely high speeds and at extremely difficult angles."

"Let's do it!" Genne responded.

JHJ smiled. "Very well. Let's start at level thirty-five." She pressed a button on her tablet and the virtual opponent served a fast corner ball. Genne returned without difficulty, dropping a ball low in front with a spin. The opponent rushed forward but didn't make it in time. The game continued for another two minutes before JHJ increased the difficulty. "Level sixty, Mr. Manning. We're just warming you up for the real game." She was monitoring his vitals as the game progressed, Anne watched, as well, half distracted with her husband and half watching the vitals. Genne was performing very well, even though he hadn't played in the last ten years.

JHJ waited for a serve to finish and paused the show. "Okay, Mr. Manning. You are barely breaking a sweat, so we're going to change the game on you. You can now hit all of the surfaces and we will be altering the ball every serve from double yellow all the way to double black. Please reassess your play every serve."

Genne was energized. "I see how it is. Bring it on!"

JHJ signaled the nurse to watch the vitals while she focused on running various game scenarios. New serve started, and the pace was significantly faster. Anne changed from cheering to simply watching in amazement. Genne was a fury of speed and power, rushing back and forth but remaining very strategic in his play. His virtual opponent also became faster and more agile. After five minutes, Genne's vitals plateaued again while his pulse remained under one hundred beats per minute.

JHJ paused the game again to discuss something with the nurse. Genne took a moment to grab a drink. Anne called out to him, making sure he was fine.

JHJ came back. "Okay, Mr. Manning. This is the last stage of the physical test. We will be increasing difficulty to the highest settings. We will continue altering how much the ball bounces, but this time we will also be altering which parts of the wall you can use for playing. Each wall has a red line that will change its position after each time you hit the ball. Do you understand?"

Genne grinned. "I understand that you must be really bored and have nothing better to do than abuse your patients, JHJ. But this is a hell lot of fun, so let's continue."

JHJ responded, "Just for that Mr. Manning, I'll throw in a few surprises for you."

The game began, faster than ever. Genne was stretched to the end of his abilities in both speed and agility. Anne changed her focus to watching Genne's vitals.

After two minutes, JHJ started to change the ball settings in the middle of the game. She altered the walls to make it more and more difficult for Genne to win and his opponent to lose. Genne began losing some of his serves and started to get frustrated."

JHJ called out a reminder, "Mr. Manning it doesn't matter if you win here! This is a physical test! Just play to get the ball!"

Genne glanced back. "But I love winning!" then bounced the ball right in front of JHJ's face, trying to startle her.

JHJ responded by placing two virtual opponents in the court, forcing Genne to play even faster, with two balls often traveling in opposite directions.

Genne tried his best but could not keep up. He started to lose his focus and became really irritated.

Genne launched himself in the air to get one of the balls, missed it, and scraped his knee instead. JHJ stopped the game and signaled to the nurse to record final vital signs. Anne rushed to her husband, worried about his injury. Genne ignored his knee and walked directly to JHJ.

"This was not a fair game."

JHJ smiled calmly, meeting his eyes, "This was not a real game, Mr. Manning." She then pointed to a small room nearby with seats and a coffee table. Genne sat down to catch his breath. Anne was curious to know the results of the physical test.

"I have some good news, some bad news, and some ugly news."

Genne and Anne looked up, slightly confused.

JHJ continued, "The good news is you played extremely well. In fact, you may want to sign up for nationals."

"What's the bad news?" Anne asked.

JHJ smiled. "The bad news is Genne can no longer play his squash buddies. He would totally dominate them and get bored."

Genne grinned, "Well that's not bad news at all. What's the ugly news then?"

JHJ spoke softly, but clearly. "Mr. Manning, while our procedure gave you much higher endurance, strength, agility, and focus, it was not able to help with your temper." She looked at Anne and said, "We'll work on that."

The room was quiet. JHJ stood and refocused. "Mr. Manning, you will be leaving our facility in a few days. I know this experience, while elating, also really stretches people both mentally and emotionally. It's a profound life change." She looked back at both Anne and Genne as they, too, stood. "Being at home should ease your mental recovery and allow you to reconnect, even ponder what's ahead for you both." She pointed to Genne's monitoring bracelet. "I will, of course, monitor you remotely and visit you weekly as promised."

Anne looked at Genne, excited. "Hon, we get to go home! You're doing well. That's excellent."

Genne returned her smile. "Finally! I missed all of the unsupervised sex without the parents watching."

Anne gave him a stern look, disapproving of the personal nature of the words spoken in front of others.

JHJ corrected her. "Anne, I'm a doctor and you're a married couple. There are no sacred topics between us." She then waved to the nurse, who approached quickly. "I'm dismissing Mr. and Mrs. Manning as of tomorrow. I know we still have some blood work and stool samples to run. Otherwise, please arrange for transportation back home and a constant security detail, as discussed."

Genne grinned. "Oh-Oh, I guess the parents will be watching after all."

JHJ responded, annoyed. "No, Mr. Manning, I'm not talking about cameras in your home. I'm talking about a few security guards watching you and your home, strictly for protection. We did just invest half a billion dollars into you. We expect you to be responsible." Her tone eased. "Just rest and recover. Pick up a hobby. Learn something new. Exercise every day. But do, please, lay low for a month or two."

Another nurse walked in with a smaller monitoring bracelet. JHJ turned to Anne. "Dear, would you mind wearing this for a little while? As you leave this facility, we want to make sure we always know where you are and that you are safe."

Anne was surprised, but agreed. "Of course, JHJ. I appreciate the thoughtfulness."

JHJ responded. "This is, of course, just a precaution. You two are so close. Our security detail will be protecting both of you."

Chapter 16: The Library

"10 and a half Beacon Street? Are you serious?" Glenn whispered to himself. He double checked his GPS. "In an age where electronic media was mainstream, physical books and magazines were so retro.

His search at a local public library showed no activity from one Lenny Small. Today's libraries offered mostly downloadable content instead of shelves of dust-collecting books, he'd discovered. Librarians were literally laughing at him asking for any hardbound classics like the one Lenny left at the murder scene. They did, however, point him to perhaps the oldest and most prestigious library in the United States, the historic Boston Athenaeum Library, founded in 1807. Its collection was predominantly paper based, and so rare that patrons had to pay a yearly subscription to access its books. He was promised that if he was looking for non-digital classics to read or borrow, this was the place.

He parked his vehicle on less-busy Park Street and walked to Beacon Street. He turned east and scanned the street, looking for the address. "I don't even know if I should look for it on the north or south side of the street," he whispered in frustration. He finally found the address and faced its bright red doors, the numerals 10 1/2 right on them. The doors themselves stood out like a fox in a hen house. The building was a beautiful eighteenth-century brownstone. The area around the doors had matching dark wooden frames with intricate carvings. Then, smack in the middle, were these strange, bright-red doors. *They should have fired the interior decorator. This looks more like an entrance to a Goth bar than a historical library,* he smirked to himself.

He pushed through the doors and was greeted by security. He showed his badge and was immediately allowed inside. He noticed the library's iconic motto, right on the wall. The Latin read *Litterarum Fructus Dulces*, which translated roughly into "sweet are the fruits of learning." His Latin from his medical training at St. George's University was rusty, but he recalled a similar Latin proverb, *Litterarum radices amarae, fructus dulces* with a somewhat different meaning: "The roots of scholarship are bitter, its fruits are sweet." He felt this second interpretation was more appropriate, although far too long for a motto.

On the right was a gift shop. He took the left, walked through a small reading room, and then entered a long hall with winding staircases on the right. He climbed to the second floor and stood still, completely overwhelmed. He now faced an impeccably preserved large library. Books filled every wall. In the middle, a row of small tables and chairs made of cherry-colored wood were filled with people carefully reading paper books. Each person wore white cotton gloves and appeared to be completely captivated by whatever they read. The room itself was very tall. In fact, a secondary walkway was installed to access books on the top parts of the bookcases. Empty wall spaces were filled with statues, painting, and other art.

He stood right in the middle of traffic, just staring, until a library staff member noticed him and asked, "Is everything alright, sir?"

Glenn's words came slowly. "Yes… it's just… well… I've never been here… In fact… I had no idea… this even existed."

The attendant smiled and replied "It's Okay. We get this all the time." Glenn's silence triggered the obvious question. "Is there anything I can help you with?"

Glenn barely remembered the purpose of his visit. "Yes, I am looking for Lenny Small." He pulled his eyes away to notice the man's name tag. Trevor was wearing khaki pants with a blue shirt, a formal black cotton vest, and a yellow bow tie.

Trevor replied, "I'm not sure we have any books by that author. I don't recognize that name. Which century was he writing in?"

Glenn's senses returned. He quickly flashed his badge and explained quietly, "Not an author. He was one of your members. I need to know how often he visited and what he was reading."

"Oh," the man responded. "Please come with me." He pointed to a side room marked Staff Only. Glenn followed him in.

Trevor approached a terminal and said, "Let me search for that name. You said Lenny Small, correct?" He typed in the name, and a list of four appeared.

Glenn peeked over the man's shoulder and saw addresses listed with the names. He pointed to one that corresponded to Lenny's apartment. "This one."

The gentlemen pressed a few more buttons and a list of books appeared. "Yes, I see. Mr. Small has been a member for about three months. It appears he had taste for British and American fiction classics."

Glenn interrupted, "Are you sure? You mean he didn't borrow any travel books from you?"

Trevor was shaking his head, dumbfounded. "Sir, we don't carry such books. This library carries mostly rare collections, some private—"

"So what was he reading?"

Trevor resumed his original statement. "He read a wide range of eighteenth and nineteenth century classics like *Tom Sawyer*, *The Catcher in the Rye*, *To Kill a Mockingbird*, *Moby-Dic*k, —"

Glenn interrupted, "To Kill what?"

The gentleman rolled his eyes. "A nineteenth-century novel written by Harper Lee." He paused, hoping Glenn would recognize the book, then provided additional details. "Lee won the Pulitzer Prize for that classic. It dealt with racial injustice and rape in early twentieth century America—"

Glenn interrupted again, "Let's focus on the last three books."

Trevor rolled his eyes again and returned to his terminal. He read the screen and announced, "Last three books are all Orwell's dystopian books: *Animal Farm*, *The Road to Wigan Pier*, and *Nineteen Eighty-Four*. That last one he renewed twice."

"That last book. I want to see it."

The man folded his hands in protest. "Do you have a warrant?"

"It's not necessary, I want to borrow it."

Trevor's arms remained folded. His voice was filled with sarcasm. "You? ... An obvious nub or worse a digiophile? On your virgin visit to this historical library? You want to borrow a 1949-printed hard-bound, limited-edition classic?"

Glenn was indignant. "Why is that so hard to believe?"

Trevor barked judgmentally "It's a lie. That's what it is."

Glenn pulled out his wallet and gave him a hundred dollars in cash.

"Well, at least you carry some money in paper form." He glanced around, took the bill, and quickly pocketed it. "Okay, here is what you have to do. You first have to buy a membership—"

Now Glenn was dumbfounded. "I have to pay to borrow this paper junk?"

Trevor continued, "I'll ignore what you just said. These are priceless pieces of history."

Glenn relented "Okay, I'll buy the bloody membership. What then?"

Trevor forced a smile "Then meet me in the second-floor gallery. In the meantime, I'll locate the book for you. It's in section PZ3."

Glenn grimaced, then backtracked downstairs to the first floor. He bought the membership and returned upstairs. He searched the large gallery room and walked across is, looking for his astute blackmailer. The gallery was a much larger area, fitted with white bookcases. The middle was filled with antique tables, couches, and Persian rugs. Unlike the other rooms he'd seen, the gallery had beautiful wide windows and arched ceilings. Columns were decorated with white busts of famous people."

He finally located Trevor in section PZ3.0793. The librarian was checking the stamps on the library card inside the front cover to confirm whether anyone had borrowed it since Lenny. No one had. Trevor said condescendingly, "I'm guessing you are not interested in any other books."

Glenn didn't bother to hide it. "Not at all…" After a pause he forced a smile and said, "… but perhaps the next time."

Trevor pointed his reading impostor to a busy desk in the back. "Let me check you out." He blushed momentarily, realizing the duality of his statement. He corrected, "I mean let me check out the book for you."

Glenn handed his new membership card to the clerk, who delicately wrapped the book in a cloth and placed it in a plastic bag branded with the library name and website. "It's your first time. Thank you for your financial support. Remember to return the book within the next two weeks."

Glenn grabbed the bag impatiently and stared at the book inside. *I have never paid $400 … wait with the bribe that's $500 … for an old piece of paper."* He promptly exited the building and speed-walked in the direction of his car. He was about to take out the book when his com device beeped.

He pulled it out and read an encrypted message from Blue. "Got a break on your search"

Glenn replied, "Great. What?"

Blue responded, "Hot informant. He will contact you."

Glenn asked, "Hot how? Bikini model?"

Blue sent, "Nah. Secret past. Knows a lot."

Glenn probed further, "How much?"

Blue replied, "Don't know. Said he wants to connect directly."

Glenn closed with, "NP. Good job."

Blue added, "Be careful."

He was about to put his com device away again when he received a call from an unlisted location. He answered, hoping it was the informant "Agent Abbot speaking. Who is this?"

The voice on the other side sounded quite upset but controlled. "I warned you, Agent Abbot, to focus on your case instead of chasing your own agenda."

Glenn recognized the voice as Innes, but he played dumb. "Who is this?"

She sounded even more irritated than before, if that was possible. "You know exactly who this is. Stop playing games."

"Oh, Innes. Hi. Good to hear from you. How can I be of help?"

"Meet me tomorrow morning at seven in my office."

"Sure, but what is this about?"

She read right through it and responded, "You are testing my patience, Agent Abbot. One more stupid comment and I'll be reporting you to Internal Affairs." She savored the silence that followed, then continued, "You are walking a very fine line, one you will regret for the rest of your career."

Glenn knew she and Mannix were well connected. He backed down. "Yes, Innes. I will absolutely meet you tomorrow morning to discuss the murder investigation."

"I warned you, Agent Abbot. The next time we meet will not be pleasant for you."

He was about to say, "Neither was our first meeting," but Innes ended the call. He knew he was in real trouble. He had overstepped boundaries during his investigation. He had forensic testing done off the books. He broke into an apartment and stole evidence. And he hired a known fugitive to gain access to classified information. He could easily get suspended, maybe even fired. He hoped to God that Innes didn't know of these actions. Perhaps he could bargain with her, give her information she didn't have in exchange for her discretion and not reporting him to Internal Affairs."

He reached his car. He sat in the driver's seat, looked at the book again, then tossed it into his back seat. His excitement fizzled and gave way to worry. He shut his car door, locked it, and headed for a nearby bar. This recent turn of events was burning him out. It was late anyway. He deserved a small break before getting flogged and fired.

I've always wanted to try a new career. Perhaps car detailing." He pondered a bit longer and smiled, *Nah... After today, I want to change my name to Trevor and be a snooty, cosmopolitan librarian...*"

Chapter 17: Alone with her Thoughts

Anne spent Saturdays cleaning. She typically kicked Genne out of the house to organize, vacuum, laundry, and plan her week ahead. It was like therapy for her. Bringing order to her immediate environment helped her feel in control. Also, it satisfied her obsessive-compulsive side to arrange everything in the kitchen cupboards. It was her favorite weekly ritual. She worked at her own pace, reflecting on the week behind as well as organizing activities for the week ahead. Genne certainly didn't mind getting away and coming back to a clean house.

She always started with the bedrooms upstairs. She changed the sheets, threw straggling clothes into a laundry basket, organized her bedside table, and set her autonomous vacuum to clean those rooms. She took the laundry baskets down to the main floor and ran her normal or delicate washer and dryer cycles. She then moved over to the living room and dining room, putting away any dishes, work items, and just reorganizing everything. Then she dusted and wiped picture frames, cabinets, and an antique flower vase, a precious family heirloom from her grandmother. Later she moved to the kitchen, placing all of the dishes in the dishwasher and also hand-washing a few delicate pieces. She reorganized her fridge, throwing out anything old and wiped all of the counters. Last, she moved to the bathrooms, putting on rubber gloves to wipe sinks and toilets.

She ended by re-programming the vacuum to clean on the main floor. Only after this was done did she relax in the bedroom with her tablet, planning the menus and calendar for the week. All along she listened and danced to her favorite Latino music.

She felt a lingering insecurity from the last few weeks. She compared herself to Innes and wondered if she too needed an upgrade like Genne. Innes was everything she thought she wanted to be: super fit, sexy, attractive, commanding, successful, and determined. Anne compared their body features, their intellects, their career successes, their personal strengths, and their life accomplishments. In all these ways, Anne found herself somehow lacking. She reflected back on her life, education, career choices, compromises, and even the opportunities she had walked away from. She started to regret so many things: not exercising more, not being more driven in her career, conceding to Genne about not having children, even buying this house. She wished for so much more.

Pulling herself from her thoughts, she went downstairs to get a drink and check on the vacuuming. Lately, the old dust buster seemed to have a mind of its own and needed to be reset regularly. She confirmed the machine did in fact finish washing and polishing all of the floors, so she parked herself on the living room couch. She smiled at seeing her grandmother's white ceramic vase. It wasn't particularly expensive or extravagant, but it was beautiful and had so much personal meaning. When her grandparents migrated from war-torn Europe, this was the only object they were able to take with them. They always talked about it to their grandchildren, how it reminded them of back home. They shared stories of wild fields with beautiful flowers that were painted on the vase, of the way they had to sneak it across the border, of various treasures they had stored in it over the years. The vase represented so many memories and happy moments for the whole family. When they passed away, they had almost no inheritance, but they knew how much Anne loved it so they left it to her. Over the years the vase had faded and chipped in a few places, but Anne's memories of these stories stayed just as vivid and just as beautiful.

Anne snapped back to the present. As she began planning the week, she reflected on the unknown life ahead of them. Would she go back to work? How would Genne cope with all the changes? Would he still be attracted to her or find her boring? Since coming back from the facility, their dinner conversations had been rather strange. Genne plunged himself into all kinds of new knowledge, including something called quantum math, some special, super-hard math used for physics.

As if regular math wasn't hard enough, she thought. She totally got lost when he tried to explain it to her.

I'm sure Innes would have gotten it, she teased herself sarcastically.

Perhaps that's what she should do. Maybe she could approach Mannix to do the treatment on her as well. She wasn't sure if her DNA was good enough, but at least that would put her and Genne back on the same level. They would both be upgraded and able to talk about quantum math and stuff like that. For a moment, she imagined herself better than Innes: smarter, fitter, and stronger. She imagined herself learning brain surgery or getting fifty PhDs and being super-smart. She imagined herself bench-pressing a midsize car. Then she laughed at that ridiculous image.

She grew quiet and reflective. Two tears ran down her left cheek as she folded her hands and whimpered aloud, "God, why did you make me like this? Why am I so weak, so broken, so dumb, such a mess?" She wasn't necessarily expecting an answer. She believed in God, an intelligent creator, a compassionate listener, but she preferred to keep him or her at a distance. She liked the idea of being in control, not some all-powerful, distant being. She did always marvel at the complexity and harmony of nature. She knew deep in her heart that she was created for a purpose. She simply didn't know what it was. So she traveled through life, creating her own. For obvious reasons, recent events made her think and question these beliefs even more. Was she just a speck in space, fading in the blink of an eye? Was she just a snowflake born for a moment to dance in the sky? Was she a vase of memories, soon to be forgotten?

She refocused on Genne. Would he outgrow her and discard her like a broken vacuum? Would he replace her for a bigger, better vacuum, capable of more sophisticated programming and fitted with great new features? She snapped herself back joking, *I bet Genne doesn't even know we have a stupid vacuum!*

Anne always trusted her heart. She always told herself she is fifty percent reason and eighty percent passion. No matter what life brought, she always resolved to move forward and allowed her passion to push her through all of the rocky parts. It was in her Italian blood, like a surge of energy that defied logic and plowed through all obstacles. She decided to move forward the best she knew how and trust that God in her infinite wisdom would steer Anne in the right direction.

Chapter 18: Round Two

Glenn's car was strip-searched once more by a handsome, armed guard at the South Boston Navy base. Once again, Glenn was teased about living in it. He smiled and moved on. Once more, he parked in a visitor area on the far side of the building. This time he backed in, just in case he had to make a quick getaway, although he knew that he just didn't really want to be there.

Once again, grumpy building guards took away his personal items, his gun, and even his shoes. And once again, one of his socks had a hole showing his protruding toe with an overgrown nail. Once more he was directed to sit down and wait. Innes made him wait twenty minutes this time, even though he arrived at seven sharp, as she requested.

When she finally arrived, she whispered something to the main guard. He nodded and pressed some buttons on his monitoring desk. He then ordered two junior guards to escort Glenn to what was no doubt a torture room. They led him through two sets of security doors, then into an elevator, then a dark hallway, and into a large, empty room. Inside was a large metal table with two bolted chairs. He noticed cameras in each corner. He sat down, worried. He waved and smiled to the camera, then thought, *This looks like a butcher table. They could cut me into pieces, and nobody would ever know it.*

Ten minutes later, the door finally reopened, and Innes marched in leaving two guards waiting behind the door. She was wearing black leather, from heavy boots all the way to her neck. Glenn decided against any of the jokes currently running through his head. She sat right across from him, fearsome and dominating.

He smiled, trying to break the ice. "Hi, Innes. How have you been?"

She ignored his distractions, waited, then spoke with force and precision. "Agent Abbot, I know you're sticking your nose into my business, where it does not belong." She asked rhetorically, "Are you investigating a murder, or my Prisoner Reform Program," but didn't pause, clearly not expecting an answer. "I have proof you are going rogue, even investigating my identity." She glared at him, looking for glimpses of acknowledgement, but Glenn avoided her eyes. She continued, raising her voice, "There is a very good reason why you do not have clearance for these matters. They are far above your pay grade." She rose and moved to force their eyes to meet. "I know you have been using illegal sources to acquire classified information," she savored saying those words. Glenn blinked. She continued, "I know you had Mr. Connor's DNA tested off the books. I also know you're searching your database for the same genetic abnormality." She enunciated the next statement, "And I know that information will take you nowhere." She paused, sat down again, and began to change her tone, "Except, of course, for a one-way trip to

Internal Affairs after which you'll be discharged, dishonourably, and most likely imprisoned." Glenn remained still and quiet, waiting for the thrashing to stop. She now looked toward the door. "You have a simple job, Agent Abbot: investigate a murder in midst of highly sensitive circumstances and government secrets. It is precisely because of these difficult circumstances that you must follow protocol, not go off on your own imaginary witch hunt.

"I do question whether you're up for the job, Agent Abbot. Your record is far from exemplary. And I hear that you live in your car after a nasty divorce and a restraining order." He resisted giving his side of the story or popping a joke.

She slammed her open hand on the table, yelling in fury, "Find the motive and person responsible for the murder! Or give the job to someone who can!" The table took a few moments to stop shaking. By then she had marched out of the room, leaving him behind.

Glenn was still in shock when the two guards escorted him back to the lobby. He received his items back, although it looked like someone searched his wallet, rearranging a couple of things. He checked his com device for signs of a break in or any sensors. He found none. Still, he was suspicious about whether they somehow put a tap on him.

He left the building in a hurry, got into his car, and started the engine. His com device started pinging. He pulled it out to read an urgent encrypted message from Blue, "China burned and gone. I'm burned. Going off-radar for a while."

Glenn swore at Innes several times and banged his steering wheel. Another message appeared, "Too hot. You owe me big." He swore again, realizing Innes's late arrival was strategic. She must have used that time to execute an intervention in China.

Glenn didn't respond. He deleted the whole history of his messages with Blue, pocketed his com device, and started doubting himself. *Why did I follow my instincts? Why all this trouble for a stupid murder case? Why did I have to focus on Innes and the Prisoner Reform Program? Maybe that had nothing to do with the murder.* In fear and frustration, he was ready to drop everything and even disappear, move to another country if he had to. Half sarcastically, he looked up to the sky, cursing it.

Just then, his com device beeped again. It was FBI forensics. Anya, the frightened analyst told him that about twenty minutes ago two senior FBI agents came in, cancelled all of Glenn's all off-books DNA tests, and deleted all of the data acquired so far. The analyst was terrified for her job. Glenn reassured her that he would take full responsibility. He wrapped up the call and cursed the sky again.

At that very moment, he received yet another encrypted message. He hesitated, expecting more bad news. The source was unknown, but he called himself Comrade. The message read, "You are looking for info about Mannix's prisoner program and Innes?"

Glenn's heart skipped a beat as he typed and sent, "Yes."

He received a reply "Meet me tomorrow at ten for tea," He re-read it, questioning, "Tea?"

He received another message with the address of a British tea house in Newton, just west of Boston. He hesitated. Considering the ordeal he just went through, was this the much-needed break or a one-way ticket to hell?

Chapter 19: A Visit

Anne and Genne knew JHJ would be arriving any minute. Their home was spotless, yet Anne was feeling very nervous. They had been back home for several days now. Genne had been growing in leaps and bounds. He exercised every day. With his boundless energy and endurance, he put on a lot of muscle and was in great shape. He inhaled all types of knowledge, including medicine, genetics, artificial intelligence, physics, and quantum mathematics. He was also unstoppable in learning languages. Every detail he consumed stuck immediately and vividly. His memory was eidetic, even photographic. He also picked up some eclectic cooking techniques and dishes. He barely needed sleep and was always busy doing something. They did spend time together, including dinners and a few romantic evenings, but overall Anne felt they had started to drift away. She was no longer the focus of his attention. His mind was always elsewhere.

The doorbell rang, and Genne rushed to open it. JHJ walked in confidently and looked around. She pointed to a nearby table, where a large man, no doubt her bodyguard, placed her equipment and left the house again, closing the front door behind him.

"How have you two been?" JHJ seemed to force herself to ask.

Anne also forced a smile. "Well. Please, sit down." She pointed to the chair beside the table. She asked hospitably, "Would you like some coffee or tea?"

JHJ responded plainly, "Water, please. Room temperature if you don't mind."

"Of course," Anne responded, and disappeared into the kitchen. She decided to warm the water slightly to her guest's liking.

JHJ began to take out some instruments, asked Genne to get up, undress to his tighty-whities, then started to assess his vitals.

Anne returned, somewhat stunned by this scene. JHJ caught her confusion in her peripheral vision, and chose to address it straight on, "Anne, please sit down. Let us be honest here." Anne sat down while Genne remained standing. JHJ continued to talk while scanning Genne. "I am, for all intents and purposes, your primary doctor now. A regular GP will have no idea how to manage Genne's physical changes and both of your mental health. As such, there is nothing you should withhold from me." She met Anne's eyes. "Certainly nothing to be embarrassed about." She pointed to Anne's monitoring bracelet, "That device you are wearing tells us far more than your location. It provides us with a real-time feed of more than one hundred health measures, including your heartbeat, blood pressure, hydration, various hormone levels, white cell blood count, and sugar levels." She paused, asked Genne to open his mouth, extracted a saliva sample, placed it in a small cylindrical container, and secured it in her case. She continued while examining Genne's back, "I can use this information to deduce a variety of information like what you ate for breakfast, when you're sleeping, and when you're having sex." Anne blushed, while Genne grinned. JHJ noticed Genne's reaction, so she added, "And for how long. I also know when you went to the bathroom, and even if you're feeling happy or upset at any specific moment." She met Anne's eyes again. "We monitor all of these things for your health and benefit. We want to make sure not only that Genne is recovering properly but also that your relationship is healthy." JHJ asked Genne to sit down, then took a small blood sample. She instructed Genne to get dressed as she placed the sample in her case.

JHJ sat down with Anne and continued her assessment, "However, one of the things that monitoring device cannot tell me is what you are thinking." She looked at Anne and asked directly, "So tell me, how is your relationship?"

Anne looked away for a moment and said, "It's different."

JHJ immediately asked, "Different how?"

Anne looked at Genne, who finished dressing and sat down at the table. "I guess I'm adjusting, then reaffirmed, "We're adjusting to the changes."

"Which ones?" JHJ asked. "Please be specific."

Anne felt a bit on the spot. "There are many of them. Genne's physical health is excellent." Now she grinned. "I know it's something silly, but I haven't seen his six-pack for ten years. Now it's back." She began to open up more, "Even his hair is growing thicker and in more places than before."

JHJ explained, "Yes, his testosterone levels are higher, causing some of these changes."

Anne continued, "He's eating like an animal and even started cooking. Just yesterday he made this excellent Mongolian chicken from an online recipe."

"What else?" JHJ asked. "I know there is something bothering you, Anne. Your heartbeat and anxiety levels rose when I asked this question."

Anne looked away for a moment, composing herself. "I guess all of these changes so quickly are quite stressful..." She glanced at JHJ, then looked away again. "I don't know..." She repeated, "I don't know..."

"You don't know what, dear?" JHJ insisted.

Anne looked back at Genne. "I don't know who Genne is becoming..." she paused to collect herself, then continued, "and I don't know if I can keep up."

"Keep up with what, dear?"

Anne blurted out, "Keep up with Genne, with all of his changes. We used to like the same things. We enjoyed Italian food, watched British mysteries or Friday nights, complained about loud next-door neighbor parties, and refused to get involved in politics. But now," she paused again, "now I don't even know what to cook for him. His tastes are changing. His interests are changing. He doesn't even fit his clothes anymore."

Genne put his arm around her, saying softly, "But I love all those things about you. That hasn't changed."

JHJ observed them silently.

Anne hid her face, "Yeah, but you are now interested in other things. How long before you get bored with me?"

JHJ stopped Genne from responding. "Anne, relationships go through all types of changes: birth of children, income shifts, buying a house for the first time, even tragedies and deaths. And yes, during these times people change. That change is what's required to adapt to new circumstances or expectations. Changes require us to evolve our relationships." She paused to focus on her next statement, "Love is the constant that does not change."

Anne's emotion was apparent, and tears came to her eyes. "I don't know who Genne is anymore." She pushed away his embrace. "I mean, what is quantum math about anyway? Why are you spending so much time on it? Why are you not watching television with me? Why…" She strained to contain her emotion.

"May I suggest you try looking at this differently?" JHJ suggested.

"Different how?" Anne still sounded confused and frustrated.

"Imagine Genne is your new boyfriend," JHJ said. "There are a number of things you already do know about him, like the car he is driving, his parents, some of his interests, but there are other things you're still learning about him." This got Anne's attention, so she continued, "Enjoy discovering new things about him, but instead of judging them to be negative or different, simply remain curious to understand what they are and how they make up who Genne is. Even go further, see if you may find those same things interesting as well. Discover a different and better way of being together."

Anne seemed to be caught off-guard, "New boyfriend…"

JHJ continued, "People in relationships complement each other's differences. They are never the same. In fact, more-successful relationships are the ones where both partners found a specific, unique role to play. You already did that before we met each other. For example, you liked to cook and clean the house on Saturdays. Genne took to family finances."

Anne looked up, wiping the tears off her face. She was starting to understand the idea.

JHJ pushed on. "Rediscover your husband, Anne. And don't let the old ways get in the way of creating something new and wonderful." She then turned to Genne, "And same to you, Genne, do not expect Anne to remain the same. Rediscover her all over again. Give her space and permission to evolve in her own way."

Genne smiled, "I will."

Anne returned his smile, "I will as well."

JHJ smiled, checked the time, and interrupted them. "Now I have a small surprise. Can you turn your television to channel three?"

Anne was caught off-guard but followed her direction.

As they turned the channel, they came upon some type of media appearance. Mannix walked up to the podium among an auditorium packed with top news providers. Numerous cameras and recording devices pointed into his face, eager to capture every sound and expression.

JHJ smiled and said, "World, embrace the new era."

Genne asked, "You mean he will announce the procedure today?"

"Not quite, Genne. He first has to make the world ready for your news. This is how he's going to do it."

They watched as Mannix smiled with all of his charm and began his announcement. "Today, dear friends, we cure cancer!" He paused dramatically waiting for whispers to subside, then continued, "Today, dear friends, I offer to you all freely, and publicly, the genetic cure for cancer." He pressed a button on his com device. He continued talking as numerous com devices began beeping throughout the room. "I just released full genetic research for all common types of cancer, as well as genetic sequences to cure them all." He paused again dramatically, then continued. "Why? My father had cancer. This disease has plagued humanity for centuries and killed billions." He became more quiet and solemn. "This information does not belong to any greedy pharmaceutical or even a governmentally policed medical practice. I have no right to keep it for myself for profit." He raised his voice. "This information belongs to the whole world. To every human being touched and affected by this terrible disease." He paused again, getting ready to wrap up and answer questions. "I also ask all medical organizations, professionals, and research bodies to remain in the spirit of this act, to develop and provide this treatment with no regard for your own benefit or profit. That is all." A flurry of questions flew from the audience.

"We don't need to watch the rest," JHJ said. "I'm sure it will be just a media frenzy, one Mannix is well prepared for."

Anne turned off the television and asked herself, but aloud, "That's amazing, but why did he do that?"

Genne heard her and answered, "Isn't it obvious? As an analogy, if you knew how to create a new clean source of power, but the selfish mega-corporations and corrupted governments resisted or banned its production, then you release the specifications to the public who, in turn, will force the government and corporations to accept the innovation."

JHJ added, "Yes, but while holding all the information and patents about its manufacturing process."

Genne pondered for a second, "A type of genetic Renaissance."

"That's a good way of describing it, Genne," JHJ agreed. "It will be similar to the fifteenth-century period where printing was discovered and information was freely shared among the masses instead of keeping information by the few."

Anne asked, "But is releasing this information irresponsible? Will people actually know how to use it safely or are we giving people keys to something they don't even understand?"

JHJ answered, "How will they ever understand if they don't have this information? This is precisely why Mannix released information about melanoma, not about how to genetically create new diseases."

Genne repeated, "He said his father had cancer. I understand why he would want to cure it. I understand why he would want to give that information to the public. And I understand why this release is necessary before releasing details of my procedure."

"We digress," JHJ said. "Let us finish this examination." She looked at Genne and continued, "Genne, the one main thing these monitors don't tell us is what you are thinking. So tell me, what's occupying your mind most of the time?"

Genne's eyes went slightly to right and up as he began, "To put it succinctly, I am trying to decide what I should do with this gift. I surmise I'm in the top fifth percentile in the human population."

JHJ interrupted "More like top tenth of a tenth of a percentile. The procedure was highly successful."

Genne nodded and continued, "This is not only a great privilege but also a great responsibility. I want to do something with this intellect."

"That's very noble," JHJ agreed.

Genne continued, "That's precisely why I've been exploring various areas of knowledge, trying to see which ones appeal to me more than others and which ones come more naturally."

JHJ agreed again, "That's excellent. Where is this taking you?"

Anne whispered, quietly, "Please, not quantum math."

Genne smiled at her comment and continued, "Actually I think I want to focus on sub-atomic genetics."

Anne grimaced, "Sub-a-what now?"

Genne explained, "It's the study of genetics on a subatomic level. It combines the biological study of genetics with subatomic physics. I find it fascinating, apparently, but also largely unexplored. I believe I can make a real difference in this field. For example, did you know that enzymes work really fast through a process called quantum tunneling, where subatomic particles are able to flip from one part of the DNA molecule to the other?"

"Great. You have a why and a what," JHJ said. "Now we just need to know how." She pondered for a moment, then continued,

"Let me see if I can share with you some educational material from H+. Some of it may be highly confidential."

Genne was visibly excited. "That would be fantastic."

"What else is occupying your mind?"

Genne answered, "I'm trying to decide what my optimal lifestyle should be, from how much I sleep, to what I eat, to my exercise regimen, to my most productive schedule, to how I manage my past thoughts and emotions."

JHJ interjected, "How is your mindfulness meditation progressing? Are you able to separate yourself from your emotions and worries?"

"For the most part, yes," he replied. "However, my mind is quite busy. I still find it difficult to focus even during meditation."

"That's fine. It takes time to learn how to disconnect yourself from everything. What else?"

"I'm trying to anticipate how life will change after my name is released to the public. I'm considering relocating somewhere more suitable and secure, yet still metropolitan."

"Interesting. Where were you thinking?"

"I was thinking Vancouver, Canada—,"

Anne interrupted, "Um... And why didn't you tell me about this?"

Genne was genuinely surprised. "Because I haven't completed my analysis—"

Anne didn't wait for the rest of the answer. "Don't you think I should be included in your analysis?"

"Hon, you know we can't stay here. We're right downtown. It will be a media circus every time we try to leave the house..."

Anne was saddened. "Do you realize you did not mention me in any of your answers to JHJ? Everything was about you! The Genne I know couldn't wait to come home and spend time with me, to talk to me, to hear about my day. The Genne I know would include me in all the important decisions, especially something like where we're going to live. The Genne I know—"

This time Genne interrupted, "was inferior, average, clumsy, and dumb. But your new Genne is far better in every way. The new Genne sees life with such lucidity—"

Anne buried her teary face in her hands. "I love the old Genne—"

JHJ interjected, seeing the direction things were going. "Did you used to fight like this before the procedure or is this new?"

Anne glared. "He has always been a self-centered child, now he just thinks he is smarter than everybody else."

Genne added, irritated, "Much smarter."

JHJ supported Anne. "Except you still have no clue about relationships. Your marriage is the closest, most intimate, most influential, and therefore the most important relationship you will ever have. I'm prescribing you to include the topic of family and marriage in your exploratory studies."

Anne grinned, "Yeah, buddy, what she said. You need training in this," she pondered for a bit then added, "and a few other things."

"Anne, please understand when a person goes through a traumatic event, such as Genne did, the brain first focuses on understanding and processing it. Right now Genne cannot help but be self-centered. His identity is re-forming. Until that process is complete, he will be quite... self-occupied." She looked at Genne. "More so than usual."

Anne motioned frantically with her hands toward Genne, "I've been training him for years. Are you saying now I have to retrain him?"

JHJ smiled, "Yes, but this time he should be able to retain more."

JHJ got up and began to pack her case. She pressed a button on her monitoring device. A moment later, her bodyguard entered the house without knocking. He finished packing her larger items and stood by the door, ready to leave. JHJ also finished packing and was about to leave.

Anne asked, anxiously, "JHJ can I... Can I ask you a personal question?"

"Of course, dear."

Anne said shyly, "Did you go through the procedure yourself?"

JHJ paused, took a deep breath as if deciding whether to answer, then did so. "No, Anne. I don't do this because I have undergone the procedure." She looked away for a second before continuing, "I do this because I fundamentally believe in it. I believe it will profoundly alter our existence and evolve our species."

"How can you be so sure?"

JHJ paused, visibly considering whether to answer. "Anne, you allowed me to enter every private area of your life, so I will be transparent with you. This time." JHJ stared deep into Anne's eyes. "My son has undergone the procedure. It saved him. It did more than save him. It was a true metamorphosis. One I will never forget, and one that makes me do what I do every day." She finished talking, but her mind remained on that thought.

"Where is your son now?"

JHJ snapped out of her trance. "I'm sorry, dear, but I really must be going. Perhaps we'll talk more another day." She moved quickly to the door, "It was good to see you both. I'll see you again in a week."

They waved goodbye as the limo drove away. She didn't look back at them.

JHJ took a deep breath, touched her com device, and said, "Innes, we need to talk. We have a problem."

Chapter 20: Unexpected Help

Agent Abbot headed to the address provided by the anonymous call. It led him to a large house in Newton, just west of Boston. It was an old mansion, converted into the British Afternoon Tea House. The place was a well-known front for a Russian mafia high-class drug-smuggling operation. The FBI kept a secret monitoring station in a small condo across the street. Over the last six months, they had been tracking numerous celebrities, politicians, and individuals of influence visiting here. In fact, the location provided so much intelligence the FBI decided to maintain its low profile and not interfere, for now.

Glenn parked his rust-bucket car at the front. It was just before ten a.m., and the place was quite empty. He entered through a pair of large, squeaky doors. The main hallway had been converted into a foyer. An attendant greeted him, and Glenn provided his name. The attendant checked for a reservation on the computer and led him to a secluded corner table. A moment later, a waiter dropped off a colorful menu that bulged slightly in one area. Curious, Glenn opened it and found a small earpiece.

As he placed the tiny device into his right ear, he heard a male voice with a heavy Russian accent, "Velcome, Agent Abbot. I appologizze we cannot meet in person, but I'm sure you understand my reasons."

Glenn responded, "I understand fine. What is your name?"

The voice on the other end responded, "Ah. My name iz not important. My information, however, iz." After a pause, the voice continued, "For now, pleaze, call me Comrade."

Glenn asked, "And is there a price to your information.., Comrade?"

The voice answered, "No price.., as long as you put that brown bittch Innes where she belongs, in high-zecurity federal prizon."

"Oh yeah? And what did she do to piss you off so much?"

"Letz just say her magical procedure comes at price of some horrible zide effects."

"And how would you know that, Comrade?"

"Becauze, dear Agent Abbot, I was one of her tezt subjects."

"Okay, I'm all ears."

"I am ex-KGB living in America as hired gun for Russian mafia. I was kought and put in jail after some radder unfortunate miztake during a job. I was convicted and given life zentence. No parole. Jail is okay, but boring. One day, the brown bittch comes in azking for volunteers for a new addiction magik treatment. I was crackhead for many years. She said I would get parole. I said why not. I signed."

Conversation was interrupted by a waiter. Glenn hadn't reviewed the menu, so he asked, "Is there anything you would recommend?"

The waiter's voice was overwhelmed by Comrade's recommendation "You muzt have Russian Earl Gray tea. And have some frezh scones with cream. I recommend blueberry."

Glenn followed Comrade's suggestion, and the waiter walked away with the order. Glenn glanced around for any watchful eyes but found none. Instead he noticed antique cabinets filled with a variety of tea pots and cups, each one intricate and different. Designs varied from more traditional British teacups to an eclectic collection of modern versions.

He asked, "Why this place?"

Comrade laughed. "Becauze, Agent Abbot, I promized you neutral place. I have good friends in there as you already know. It's plaze FBI iz watching. And you know we know you are watching. So everybody is watching."

Glenn smiled. "Let's continue. What happened next?"

"Lies. No magik. More like mutation. My body changed in very strange wayz. Unbearable pain. Eventually I even went crazzy…"

"Wait! Mutated how?!"

The voice on the other side grew quiet. Eventually, answers followed, "That bittch. She zaid nothing about thiz. My body was rejecting the treatment. Muscles felt on fire. My skin changed color. So much pain! Conztantly! No amount of morpheme helped. No sleep for weeks. Drove my crazzy."

Silence followed. Glenn sensed his informant was trying to regain control over his emotions. "Did they release you and got you help?"

"Release no. I didn't read the zmall print. Bittch had me sign my life away. I had to stay on compound till treatment finished and the bittch decides when itz finished."

They were interrupted again by the waiter bringing tea, strainer, raw sugar, and cream. Glenn waited for his informant to calm down.

"They didn't stop. They run more tezts. Months. Lotz of drugs to sedate me. Some things got better but lots of surgeries." Glenn heard quiet weeping before, "They took my legs. They cut them off, buztards!"

"I'm so sorry Comrade. Sorry, did you say they amputated your legs?"

"That iz why they must pay!"

"So how did you get out?"

"My KGB friends. They found me. They attacked my transport to another fazility. They hide me now."

"Do you have any proof or information about what happened?"

"Agent Abbot I have something far more uzeful. Check for the envelope under your chair. You will find a file there."

Glenn reached under his seat and pulled out a large, brown envelope. He ripped the top and reached inside. He was surprised to pull out a prisoner file. "You are giving me your file? Or the file of another prisoner in the program?"

"Oh Agent Abbot, I give you something far more valuable."

Glenn flipped the file to see the front. On the cover was the name: Innes Tannah.

At the same time, the voice continued, "I give you something you can uze. I give you the bittch Innes."

"Wait! What?"

"The brown bittch was one of us! All her files were deztroyed. I acquired this one at great perzonal price."

"You mean she was one of the original prisoners in the program? Like patient zero?"

"One of the first for sure. File has more. Now enjoy your tea. Just be careful. The bittch has friends in high places. Even FBI." The voice disappeared suddenly.

Glenn glanced around again, and quickly placed the file back in the envelope. At that moment the waiter arrived with two blueberry scones, some cream, and homemade jam. He decided it was safer to open and examine this file back in the office. He knew this file would break his case wide open and give him leverage over Innes.

He took his time to finish the tea and scones. He left the house, stopped on the sidewalk to drop his earpiece, then stepped on it, destroying it. He glanced around, then got into his car and drove away quickly.

Chapter 21: A Dream

Is this a dream, a vision, or a memory? The thought drifted in Genne's half-awake mind. It was three a.m. He was shivering and sweating, trying to fall asleep. He could see himself lying on that special hospital bed in Mannix's facility. He wonders if the bed was an object or a living organism. He feels its energy. He remembers the comfort. He recalls the sedative slowly seducing his body into compliance and relaxation. He struggles to see Anne's face as he fades out. His body is limp, yet his mind is alert and clear this time. He can sense people around him. He can hear Mannix. He senses Anne not too far from him.

What's this? Two strangers approach, carrying something. It, too, has energy. Great energy. It's pulsating, powerful. He senses it getting closer. He is helpless as the object nears him, as the tentacles of the bed restrain him, as this liquid energy slowly enters his bloodstream. He struggles, so afraid. Yet his body does not move. He calls out for help as he feels the liquid traveling through his arm. He senses great danger. He screams! Yet his body does not move. The liquid now works through his entire body. He struggles to fight it as it saturates him. He begins to fade out again. He senses his body being moved to another room. He drifts away, hearing a strange voice "He is ready for phase two. Place him in the pod."

~ * ~ * ~ * ~

Is this a dream or a memory? another thought crosses Genne's mind on a sleepless night. The vision changes. He is no longer on a strange bed. Instead he is in a … he struggles to recognize it… a cocoon? He is confused. He is looking from outside in. In front of him is an egg-shaped pod. Walls are made of a single substance. He notices the letters FM2030 on it. He has no idea what that means. He wants to look inside, but he can't find any glass. Frustrated, he tries to open it. His hand goes right through it as if the pod is a hologram. He decides to look inside and submerges his face in the wall. He pulls right out in terror. It's his face inside. His body. His heart beating. He looks inside again, suppressing his fear. He can sense the liquid energy pulsating stronger and stronger. Is he a ghost looking at his own body?

He senses something is going wrong. The liquid power grows stronger as his heartbeat gets weaker and weaker. He reaches out to wake his body in the pod. It is of no use. He is but a ghost, sentenced to observe his own demise. He looks inside again. The liquid penetrates every organ, every cell, every molecule in his body. It's pulsating stronger and stronger, overpowering. The heart tries to fight back, but it is far too weak.

Then suddenly the energy pulse dies. He is relieved that the pain and danger are gone. The heart grows hopeful and stronger. Suddenly, a blast of power blinds and overwhelms the scene. The liquid energy, like a fuel igniting an explosion. The body is on fire. Every cell screaming in pain, being burned. The ghost screams out for help, but no sound comes out. The body is blazing blue. The horror! The ghost leaves the pod to look for help, but finds only dark emptiness all around. He returns, sensing the end is near. He is frantically reaching to disconnect strange plugs and stop this torture, but he can only watch. He closes his eyes as the ghost floats into the air above the pod. He can only sense the heartbeat slower and weaker as the body burns. A tear runs down the ghost's face. It rolls down the cheek, then detaches and falls through the air. As it hits the pod, the heart stops. Genne is no more. The ghost, too, fades away.

~ * ~ * ~ * ~

Is this a memory? The fearful thought burns Genne's mind as the nightmare continues. The ghost returns as the heart awakens once more. He hovers above his body and the pod. The senses return to his body. He senses his heart beating, stronger and stronger. Yet this time, its rhythm matches the pulse of the liquid energy inside. It's strange. They beat as one. The energy is making the heart beat stronger. Stronger. Even Stronger. Now stronger than it was ever before. It's overpowering his heart. It's controlling it. It envelops it. It saturates it.

The ghost now feels the heartbeat even within its temporal shape. The energy pulls him closer. The ghost resists. It tries to escape, fights for freedom. The energy pulse grows even stronger. A tentacle-like arm reaches out of the body and grabs the shape. The body trembles momentarily. Other voices in the room emerge. The ghost panics and tries to pull away with all of its might. The energy pulses, stronger yet again. The tentacles pull it closer and closer to the body. The ghost does not recognize the body, refuses to return, and lets out a ghastly scream. Other voices grow louder. The ghost is forced and tormented back into the body. It's beginning to fade out of existence as quickly as it appeared in the first place. It grasps for last moments of being. The tentacle squeezes its throat and chest. It struggles to breathe. The energy overpowers it. It releases its last breath, slowly fading away.

~ * ~ * ~ * ~

Genne wakes, gasping for air as if this nightmare brought him to the point of death and then brought him back to life. He sits on the bed sweating and scared. He wonders *Was this a dream, a vision, or a memory?*

Chapter 22: Ghost of the Past

Agent Abbot did not want to go back to his office. He was too suspicious about how Innes knew everything about his investigation. He was going to take further precautions in case he was being observed. He drove for a while, watching to see if he was being followed. He eventually parked his car in a subway parking lot at Braintree, a small, quiet suburb south of Boston, perhaps most known for being the scene of the infamous 1920 murders by U.S. anarchists. He took the red line to Downtown Crossing, where he switched to the yellow subway line. He checked again to see if he was being followed. He got off at the next stop at State, right by the Old State House, scene of the Boston Massacre, then switched to the blue line. He walked to the very front of the train, where he was the only one in the cabin. He took it all the way to Bowdoin, then walked a block on street level till he re-entered the subway red line on Charles. He traveled to Park Street, then walked to the Isabella Gardner Museum. Although not typically following this particular maze, he visited this famous museum at times when he needed to focus and think. He parked himself in a secluded corner seat at the Café G and ordered a black forest ham sandwich with some local beer.

He glanced around, but the café was pretty empty at three in the afternoon, one hour before closing. The only customers were with college students, no suspicious men dressed in black raincoats with well-hidden machine guns. Ironically, the museum's namesake was also known as Mrs. Jack, which by itself was a frequent topic of jokes with his office colleague. "Jack, if you had any idea what your wife has on the dessert menu..."

He slowly pulled out the file from the envelope. He hid its contents inside a local newspaper and began reading. Born thirty-five years ago, her mother was an Egyptian translator, her father a high-ranking Japanese military diplomat. She grew up in Tokyo. She was the only child of what seemed to be a very difficult marriage. Her mother reported abuse several times, but due to father's stature, her pleas were ignored. She tried to leave and even run away with her daughter, but each time was caught. What followed each time was a severe beating from her husband. Innes grew up angry and rebellious. She was brilliant in school as well as martial arts studies but rejected all forms of authority. As a teen, she caused a major scene by barging into her father's work during an important government meeting, chastising him in front of high officials for how he treated her mother. He in turn retaliated to this blatant and unacceptable show of disrespect by beating and disowning her.

At the age of sixteen, she convinced her mother to run away then turned to streets as an act of anarchy and defiance. Not wanting to submit to any authority, she freelanced as an assassin. Five years later, she was well established and nicknamed Aka, meaning red in reference to the brutal murder scenes she left behind. She operated anonymously via an untraceable digital account. She was stealthy and extremely efficient. Being independent, she did not care who her target was. Except for its gender. It had to be a man. The next two years were really busy for her, as the original Yakuza families battled for control with the newer and smaller Sumiyoshi-kai and Inagawa-kai families… testing the oldest and largest Yamaguchi-gumi family. She regularly took five to eight contracts at the same time and earned a small fortune.

She was relentless, first stalking her prey for days and watching their every more. She observed her targets both in business and home situations. The more her target was abusive to his subordinates and family, the bloodier their murder. She took the time to paint the murder scene with Japanese symbols listing the sins of her victims, both crime related as well as more private ones. She adopted the Yakuza tradition of Irezumi tattooing. After each assassination, she got a tattoo of the greatest sin of her victim. She relished enduring the traditional and extremely painful Irezumi procedure, inserting ink directly under the skin with hand-made tools instead of painting on top of it with far less painful electric needles.

As the Yakuza family wars subsided, her business turned to a few incorruptible police and government officials. Her contracts were fewer and less bloody. Until one day, at age twenty-four, she received an assassination contract that she did not expect, or perhaps had waited for all of her adult life. She abruptly stopped taking other contracts, disappeared, and plotted for her life-defining masterpiece. Four months after receiving her contract she executed the most horrible assassination to date and one for which she refused payment. She brutally murdered her father with more than 120 strategic cuts and incapacitating stabs. She then wrapped him, still partly alive, in 120 meters of burial canvas where she had pre-written 120 sins of his life. She then set him on fire. The assassination was highly publicized in both local and international media. After the fact, she publicly exposed numerous documents of her father's family's involvement in highly unethical biological and chemical warfare research, something called Unit 731.

Once more she vanished. She reappeared a year after, this time in a Chicago hospital overdosed on crystal meth. The CIA and FBI played their cards and she remained on U.S. soil as an informant instead of being extradited back to Japan. Being turned into the Japanese authorities would surely result in a death sentence. She traded her Yakuza information for her freedom until one day she snapped, brutally killed twenty-three agents guarding her safe house, then escaped. Eventually, she was tracked down and placed in a high-security federal prison. She was far too valuable as an asset to be executed, however, she was far too volatile to be out in the public. For the next four years she remained incarcerated while the FBI and CIA tried to rehabilitate her. Their determination turned to desperation, so they allowed her to turn back to cocaine. Then they kept using her, trading drugs for key information they needed. She became a ghost of her former self.

One day, Mannix showed up at the prison. He was truly captured by her life story. He singled her out for the Genetic Prisoner Reform Program. They made a very strong connection. Mannix's charismatic, non-authoritarian leadership approach was completely different from anything she had ever experienced. She agreed to join the program, looking for a new start in life. Mannix convinced the FBI that this way she would also be more willing to share information. She was one of the very first program test cases, a very successful one at that. She came out of the program reborn. She completely cooperated with authorities and turned over all of the Yakuza information she possessed. She was free to live a semi-normal life while remaining under government monitoring and supervision. Mannix hired her immediately to work for the program. Initially, she oriented and converted new prisoner patients. Mannix treated her as the daughter he never had. She, in turn, reciprocated with the respect and obedience she had learned from her mother. She left her old life and embraced her new one. As a conscious, self-defining act, she underwent a very painful procedure to remove all of her Irezumi tattoos. She no longer carried the sins of her victims. She did, however, carry physical scars that replaced them, why she always wore clothing that discreetly covered most of her body.

With her new gifts, she finished a ten-year Harvard human genetics program in two years, then joined Mannix's newly formed H+ company, and focused her life on human genetic modification. Mannix promoted her as program administrator and she continued to rehabilitate life-sentence prisoners like herself. This was her redemption, helping others to get out of the horrors she was all too familiar with. However, after a few months, she found it quite taxing emotionally to work directly with prisoners, especially ones whose crimes reflected her own violent past.

The file information ended a few months earlier. Glenn checked some photos, her birth certificate, and other, less-relevant information. He then came across a reference to Lenny Small, one of the first prisoners Innes initiated and converted for the program. They knew each other well. She personally supervised his treatment and recovery. It was the first time she helped someone instead of murdering them. She continued checking on Lenny after recovery, but their relationship remained professional. Lenny had feelings for her, but they were never returned. In fact, a few months after Lenny was released to freedom, Innes requested another program manager continue monitoring him instead. She distanced herself and ignored all of Lenny's requests for contact. It was common for people going through traumatic events to anchor themselves to the people treating them, Glenn knew, even idealizing them as heroes or developing intimate feelings for them.

Glenn was disappointed. He had found a connection between Lenny and Innes, but nothing reliable as a motive for this brutal murder. Nothing to explain the book. Nothing to explain the note on the wall in blood. In fact, her being George just didn't make sense. He was missing something. Perhaps something only Innes knew about Lenny. He exhaled heavily, *This is not a conversation I'm prepared to have with Innes, the destroyer of worlds."* He grinned at that last part he had added jokingly. *And she will be pissed to find out how I know about any of this.*

He packed the file together and placed it back in the envelope. He finished his sandwich, just noticing the unique taste of sweet and salty gruyere cheese. He scanned his surroundings again. The café was almost empty. With a few minutes until the four o'clock closing time, staff members were already wiping tables, stacking bright red chairs, taking out garbage, and cleaning the floors. Some of the red ceiling lamps were already turned off, signaling to visitors it was time to leave. Glenn backtracked to the subway, this time taking the shortest path back to Braintree station. He drove back to the office, checking again to see if he was being followed.

He wondered where to hide the file. It would not be safe in the office, and he sure didn't want to turn it over to the agency's hands. He resolved to hide it in the only safe place he knew, his car. He pulled over into a well-covered, forested area just off the road, opened his trunk, unloaded its contents, removed the fabric lining from its base, then taped the file to the plastic base. He placed the fabric lining, ensuring the file was not visible through it. He re-packed the trunk and continued driving. *Dear Innes, we're now playing with even hands. Let's see your next move.*

Chapter 23: Cracked Reflection

Anne heard a loud crash in the bathroom and rushed in, alarmed. Genne pretended nothing happened, even though the mirror was completely shattered, and he was pulling pieces of glass out of his fist.

"What the hell happened?" she asked, straining to retain her composure.

"Nothing!"

"What did you do, Mr. Superman? Break the bathroom mirror with your eye laser beam?"

He grinned in appreciation of her sarcasm. "No." He hesitated to provide an explanation, "I didn't like what I saw there."

"I know! Millions of dollars of genetic engineering and still inferior to an average woman. Would you like some makeup?"

Genne's smile widened. "Funny, but that's not what I meant—"

She interrupted, wagging her finger at him, "That's no excuse to break a perfectly good mirror!" She reached out and helped him to wash his wounded hand. She lowered her voice and continued softly, "So, are you going to tell me what really happened? And don't lie to me…" She met his eyes, trying to read his emotion. "You know I will get royally pissed off if you're planning to redecorate this bathroom without involving me."

He avoided her eyes. "This face reminds me … reminds me too much about who I was …"

She grimaced. "Who you were? You mean the sexy, rugged, slightly overweight marketing geek?"

Genne said quietly, "Just average …"

Anne's face froze slightly. She stood up in front of Genne, her arms resting on her waist. "Average how?"

"Hon, do you understand the responsibility and the opportunity the universe placed on my shoulders?"

"To break the bathroom mirror … ?"

He ignored her response. "This new reality changes everything. It radically changes my future. It will also have a radical impact on the future of human evolution."

She continued to distract him. "Not before you install a new mirror."

He continued with his line of thinking. "My face is the one thing that hasn't changed. It's a constant reminder of who I was in the past, my limitations, my faults, my failures—"

She interrupted him again "—it was a really good bathroom mirror."

"Who cares about the mirror? It can be easily replaced. I am talking about the enormous pressure ahead of me and how my past is holding me back—"

She was getting irritated. "Your past does not hold you back—"

Genne walked out of the bathroom, through the living room, and toward the first aid kit in the kitchen. He paused in front of Anne's grandma's vase. "It's just like this stupid old vase. Here we have a newly furnished, modern home—" He added, looking back as Anne walked out of the bathroom to follow him, "… yet smack in the middle of it all there is this ancient, dirty piece of non-functional clay."

"How dare you? This heirloom came from my dear grandma. It is precious and beautiful—"

This time Genne interrupted her, "It is hideous and it's holding you back. I can't believe you don't see it." He paused, noticing a tear on Anne's cheek.

"I've spent my whole life confined by my limitations. But this is no longer the case. Mannix liberated me! I feel energized. I feel like I can take on the whole world. I feel like nothing can stop me." he became highly animated. "Yet every time I look into that stupid mirror, I am reminded of who I was, and the more I look at it the more I hate it. I am so much more now. I am untethered, no longer defined by my past, yet the past is staring back at me." He looked away and added carefully, "If I could change my face, I would."

Anne said coldly, "You want to get plastic surgery for your face?"

"Yes I do. And I want to change my name. I don't want to be defined by anything in my past. It doesn't reflect what I'm capable of or what I'll accomplish in the future. I don't want people to judge me by my past." He looked around the living room and continued, "And I don't like this house. It's insufficient for the work I see ahead for my life. It lacks space, functionality, security, and it's in the wrong geographical region. Living in a milder climate would allow me to be more productive throughout the year. All of these things are holding me back."

Anne's eyes were filling with tears as she said, "What else is holding you back? What about me?" She tried to find his eyes. "Am I holding you back?"

Genne didn't turn, and he didn't answer.

Anne's sadness turned to fury, "You piece of shit. I am the one that's holding your fragile superego in one sane piece."

She grabbed her jacket, slipped on her shoes and left the house, crying.

Genne didn't follow. He simply whispered to himself, "You were…"

Chapter 24: Finding George

Glenn parked himself on an old park bench with a twelve-inch spicy Italian sausage dressed for a heart attack… bacon, fried Spanish onions, spicy Havarti, mayo, and a collection of vegetable-based toppings. In his other hand he held a small bag with a recently borrowed, limited-edition 1949 printed relic *Nineteen Eighty-Four*, written by G. Orwell. In his teeth he carefully balanced a cup of dark-roasted goodness. He hesitated for a moment, trying to decide how to juggle it all, then put the bag down. First, he used the newly free hand to liberate his coffee and place it beside the bag. What followed was the moment he had waited for more than a week. There were many street vendors in Boston. However, his favorite came out only when the New England Patriots played at home. This sandwich was not only a ritual for Glenn, it was the closest thing for him to a religious experience. He grabbed the grub with both hands and stuffed a third of the sandwich into his mouth. He savored the symphony in his mouth. He took a deep breath and stretched his hands upward, ensuring the sandwich remained safe at all times. Several birds were sitting in branches above him.

He took another bite of sausage heaven, then gently placed it beside the coffee. A cyclist breezed past, startling him. He jerked, tipping the coffee over onto the bag. He immediately reached out to save his coffee. Next he lifted the bag, shaking off the brown liquid. He wiped his hands on his pants, then carefully reached inside the bag. He wasn't sure what would happen if he somehow damaged the book. He suspected Trevor from the Boston Athenaeum Library would be quite upset. He reflected, pondering if he should have purchased some of those white gloves he saw other people use in the library. He quickly ignored the voice of reason in his head and proceeded to pull out the book. Thankfully, the bag served as an effective shield from the liquid. There were no traces of coffee on the book.

He began to flip the first few pages of the book, looking for some clues. He was hoping he wouldn't have to read the whole thing. He passed the table of contents and landed on the first page. Immediately, his eyes traveled to the bottom of the page. He recognized these words from Lenny's apartment mirror: "Big Brother is watching you." He read a few pages of the book and learned this piece of dystopian fiction imagined a world where everyone was constantly watched by a government body called Big Brother.

He continued reading the book, looking for more clues. He flipped a few more pages, then reached out for a sip of coffee. He paused again, finding another interesting section in the book. He pulled the cup away from his lips, noticing some coffee on the exterior of the cup. He noticed a drop forming at the base, about to launch itself toward the book directly below. He pulled the antique away just in time, literally inches from its demise. He placed the coffee back on the bench and focused on the words in capital letters "WAR IS PEACE. FREEDOM IS SLAVERY. IGNORANCE IS STRENGTH." This apparently represented the slogan of the dictatorship in this piece of nostalgic fiction. He wondered about the significance of these words. He placed the book in his left hand, flipping pages to find where this piece of propaganda was explained. With his right hand, he reached for the hot dog without looking. He managed to feel his way to it, but not without getting its saucy toppings all over his hand. He gorged on this culinary street art, then placed the remaining piece of the dog back on the bench beside him. He reached out to flip more pages of the book but stopped himself realizing fried onion oil would not look very attractive on a 1949 printed classic. He licked his fingers clean, then reached out again. He hesitated. Trevor from the library would not have approved of that either. He wiped his saliva-wet fingers on his pants, then proceeded to flip a few more pages. He struggled to connect the meaning of these words with his case. He decided to move on.

He got a bit restless and began to examine the book itself. He flipped the book over to examine its well-worn seams. As he did that, a piece of paper fell out of the book. He carefully opened the book to where he thought the note had been hidden. The book split open to page 270. He placed the open book on his lap, then reached for the paper that had fallen to the ground. He unfolded it and read.

> *My name is Lenny Small and I'm about to commit a murder. The last two years have been the realization of a dream I never imagined possible. I was ripped out of the deepest hell and rescued into heaven. Yet heaven, as we know it, is not what it seems, and no matter how much my saviors tried, they could not simply erase my past. I have come to the realization that, at least for me, the dream of heaven cannot*

be realized by simply evolving. Regardless of changes to my body, the ghosts of the past haunt my mind and soul. I am caught in the middle, a new hell in itself. I anguished, struggling to rebirth my soul. I now know my dreams of traveling to wonderful places will never be realized. I have also accepted my love for Innes will never be reciprocated. And so I turned to the comfort and wisdom of writings such as these you currently hold. I must say they not only consoled me, they also brought clarity to my heartfelt pain. My big brother constantly watching me denies the truth of my condition, while I came to accept the duality of my being. I have no choice but to aid those who traveled with me and force my saviors to realize their salvation is both a gift and a curse. So I choose to commit another heinous, murderous act of my past to save a future for those like me. And I know my double-thinking big brother will act in their interests to protect their enterprise and make it all disappear, regardless of the abundant evidence I'll leave behind.

That is why I wrote this note and fate has chosen you to expose it. I charge you with an unfortunate but necessary responsibility to provide this evidence to the world.

The hell with the rabbits!

This war is my peace. The freedom they offer is slavery. I would have preferred dying ignorant.

Lenny

Glenn's mind raced as pieces fell into place. He looked at the book's spine, reading the name of the author, George Orwell, and realized *George is not a person.* He paused to correct himself *Okay, it is a person. A dead person.* Again he felt underwhelmed about his conclusion. *Lenny's George is George Orwell, the author of this book, not some kind of murder mastermind or accomplice. It seems, if this note is authentic, that Lenny's brutal murder was a statement to the people managing the Prisoner Reform Program. They are the ones monitoring him like a big brother. But what the hell was double thinking?*

He picked up the book and turned it around. At that same time, a large crow launched a ballistic attack at Glenn. He moved his body to dodge, but it was too late. Its gross missile landed on the pants where the book had rested only a moment ago. Glenn cursed at the bird and his pants. He took the napkin and wiped off the bird's excrement, then returned to the book, still open to page 270. His eyes immediately drew to the word he was questioning, DOUBLETHINK. It meant "the power of holding two contradictory beliefs in one's mind simultaneously and accepting both of them." He tried to process the concept and its relevance. Perhaps it was how Lenny tried to explain the dogma he was taught in the program. *How could someone be so convinced they could evolve the body without first evolving the heart and mind? How could someone deny his part and completely become someone new altogether?*

Glenn took out his com device to look up more information on George Orwell. He found a wiki describing the man as a soldier trying to reconcile a deep sense of justice within the context of an imperfect Anglican religion. All of this amidst a backdrop of war and political turmoil, creating a world of existential dystopia. A few personal quotes really stood out: "Happiness can exist only in acceptance;" "There are some ideas so wrong that only a very intelligent person could believe in them;" "The essence of being human is that one does not seek perfection;" and finally "War is war. The only good human is a dead one." Glenn paused to absorb and process the writer in his context. *Is that what Lenny was feeling?*

What didn't make any sense is Lenny's claims that Mannix ignored his degradation and warnings. They would have monitored his activity the same as they did with Scott Connor and other prisoners in their program. This wasn't a sudden change. It didn't appear that Lenny suddenly became unstable. *Why didn't they intervene?* He sighed, landing on an inevitable and unfortunate conclusion. There is only one person who would be able to provide these answers. He twisted his mouth. "The browwn bittch," he said, quoting his Russian informant from the tea house. He closed the book with the note back inside it, placed it inside his interior jacket pocket, then looked up, groaning. The one person who could provide these answers would likely end his career and perhaps his life. He thought to himself *Ready for round three…*

Chapter 25: More Secrets

Innes was visibly upset while preparing for her weekly update with Mannix. It felt like her world was suddenly crumbling. JHJ had warned her that their new patient, Genne Manning, was having significant issues reconnecting to his life and home environment. She predicted he would leave his wife and recommended bringing him into a secure facility for extended rehabilitation prior to any public appearances. This was terrible news, especially days before Mannix's next scheduled appearance and the announcement of the procedure. She was in damage-control mode, and she took failure like this very personally.

Perhaps worse, her surveillance of Agent Abbot and his investigation into Lenny's brutal murder revealed a particularly private and nasty detail. He had somehow come into possession of a highly classified personal file about Innes. Her dark past, one she desperately tried to tear away from, kept creeping back into her life. The FBI agent now possessed a significant piece of leverage against her. Related to that, Agent Abbot had made a point of avoiding his office since their last encounter. This made surveillance much harder. She was concerned what other information he had been able to uncover and why he chose not to reveal it even to the agency he was so loyal to.

Finally, she feared what she must do to recover her personal file from Agent Abbot. She doubted she could coerce Glenn to surrender it voluntarily. Their past encounters were somewhat lacking in trust and congeniality. He would use this as an opportunity. Would she have to betray Mannix and reveal details of the prisoner rehabilitation program, or would she have to betray herself and resort to a violent path, one she had divorced herself from and now found completely appalling?

She sat down on a small mat, quietly meditating and settling her mind before the meeting. The light in her room dimmed. She counted seconds as she took out her contact lenses and placed them in the small box before her. A small light began to flicker. She motioned, and Mannix appeared on the screen.

She bowed and greeted him in Japanese, "Ohayou gozaimasu, Mannix sensei."

Mannix grinned. "You're not going to give up these formalities, are you?"

She answered, still in a submissive, bowed position, "Not as long as you remain my sensei."

He released her, "I accept your sign of respect. I hope the bond we have formed is that of a friend and a colleague, not simply a teacher and a student or a boss and an employee."

She raised her body, replying, "I would be honored."

He lightened the mood, "I tell you what … you and me … let's play squash next Wednesday. I know nobody can beat you in that court, but I want to try anyway."

She nodded. "I will be torn between embarrassing you in front of the staff and honoring you by discretely letting you win."

"It would dishonor me if you let me win, dear Innes. Remember, I'm not Japanese."

She responded confidently, "Then it will be my pleasure to beat you in a fair game."

"How is our Agent Abbot progressing? Is he causing any further trouble?"

"He was," she replied. "We met. We reached an understanding. His investigation continues. I will deal with him if he causes any more trouble."

Mannix grinned. "I know you can be very persuasive when you need to be, Innes. I already feel sorry for him." Then he added "Very well. Keep me updated."

"I'm afraid we have a more troubling matter to attend to."

"Yes, I read JHJ's report about Genne. I, too, am concerned."

Innes continued, "Perhaps we released him from our care too quickly. Unlike prisoners, we expected his recovery would be more effective in a familiar home environment. Unfortunately, this amplified and accelerated his detachment process."

"Yes, I saw the latest recording of their fight at home. We need to bring Genne in for additional reprogramming and rehabilitation. It will be for their safety."

"How about Anne?"

"Right now, her presence is adding complexity to this recovery. Let's separate them first to provide a more controlled healing environment for Genne." Innes nodded in agreement as her boss continued, "We may introduce her later. I'm sure you can provide her with a suitable explanation. I'm afraid right now she is more of a liability than a help." Innes nodded again. Mannix noticed and continued, "Very well, then, we have a plan. Let's execute it quickly before things escalate even further."

"I'm already on my way to assist in the extraction."

"I'm not sure that's necessary, Innes. I'm sure JHJ can handle the matter quite well."

"This is my failure sensei Mannix. I need to oversee its correction."

Mannix paused, considering her response, then agreed. "Very well, if you feel personally compelled to do so."

Innes bowed slightly. "Thank you."

Mannix spoke carefully. "I am worried about you, Innes. Your vitals over the last forty-eight hours have been very erratic. Do you want to tell me what's the matter?"

"It's a personal matter. I assure you, it will not impact my work."

"I understand if you don't wish to tell me, but please understand I'm very concerned about your well-being, as your employer, your mentor, your doctor, and your friend."

Innes hesitated, and her pulse spiked. She noticed and focused to regain control. "I promise you that by the end of tomorrow this matter will be closed and my vitals will return to normal."

Mannix concluded she must be referring to issues with Genne Manning. He didn't press the subject any further. Instead he reassured her, "Very well, but if your signs worsen or do not resolve in the next forty-eight hours, I'll want you to come into the facility for closer observation and rehabilitation. You are far too important to our research, to this organization, and to—"

Innes rushed in, not waiting for Mannix to finish, "I will, sensei."

Mannix paused, stunned. Innes had never interrupted him, not in their entire patient and professional relationship. He waited quietly as she realized what happened.

He cut into the silence, "Innes, this behavior is very uncharacteristic of you." Then he insisted, "I will need you to come into our facility for a while. We can better treat you while you recover and regain balance."

Innes pleaded, "May I at least redeem my honor and extract Genne Manning?"

Mannix pondered, then conceded, "Very well, but please understand your honor is not in question. Extract Genne and bring him with you."

Innes exclaimed, relieved, "Thank you, sensei."

Mannix paused before making an unexpected request. "I need you to do something else for me."

"Of course, sensei. What is it?"

Mannix explained, "I had a bit of time to look up your Agent Abbot. Would it be possible for you to acquire a sample of his blood? Use your agency connections if necessary."

She was confused. What Mannix requested was a breach of their typical process and patient-privacy policies. Nonetheless, she was already planning to run into Glenn Abbot that very night. "Of course, sensei. But," she paused, unsure of how to pose her question "I'm just unclear about the reason for this request."

Mannix answered mysteriously, "Let's call it personal curiosity."

Chapter 26: The Altercation

Anne sneaked into her home through the back door beside the kitchen. She moved quietly, hoping Genne wasn't home. She planned to pack a few things and get away for a week or so. The break would give them both space and, hopefully, remind Genne how much he needed her. This worked well the last time they clashed over whether to have children.

She stepped into the kitchen, quietly closing the door behind her. She peeked into the corner of the living room. The lights were on, but she didn't see any movement and didn't hear any sounds. She did, however, notice from the corner of her eye that the armchair typically in that area was missing. She found that odd, but not important in the current circumstances. She slipped off her shoes and ran upstairs, moving softly and quickly like a cat. She moved carefully through the dark hallway into her walk-in closet, right next to the master bedroom. There was no sign of Genne anywhere. She grabbed a large travel bag and began to pack it with clothes, toiletries, makeup, and a couple pairs of shoes. Simultaneously, she was on the lookout for any movement or sounds. She was almost done when she heard a sharp breaking noise downstairs. She cut her packing short and began to slither quietly down the stairs.

* * *

Glenn's com device was beeping, but he ignored it. He was tired both physically and emotionally. It was late. He was heading to a secluded area in the huge Port of Boston where he parked every night to sleep. He manually silenced the second com request, noticing it was from a restricted address. In the background, however, his brain was asking a nagging question: *Who was trying to reach him?* The area was dark and empty at this late hour. The com device beeped again. The address again was restricted. Regardless, he chose to answer it.

On the other end, a female voice sent shivers down his spine. "I know you have my file." Glenn's silence was a sign of acknowledgement, so the voice continued, "You will surrender it to me without any questions."

Glenn bit his tongue. "The thing is, Innes," He second guessed himself, "and I'm guessing it's Innes on the other side or else this conversation is really awkward." Then returned to his original thought, "The thing is, Innes, I do have a lot of questions I will need you to answer first."

Innes constrained her anger. "This is not a negotiation or an exchange, Agent Abbot. This is a demand. Your refusal will have tragic consequences."

Glenn played his hand carefully. "I understand you are angry. How about a coffee?"

Innes hissed furiously, "You leave me no choice," and hung up.

Glenn had a bad feeling about this. He decided to call Jack, but his co-worker didn't pick up. He hung up, unsure of how to proceed. He called back, this time leaving a message. "Jack, this is Glenn. Sorry for a long, cryptic message. I may be over my head with this strange murder investigation. As insurance, I'm entrusting you with few key details. The murderer is one Lenny Small, previously a participant in Mannix's Genetic Prisoner Reform Program. My investigation has been extremely difficult. I'm even getting personal threats from Innes Tannah, Mannix's program administrator. Anyway, Lenny committed the murder intentionally. It was a statement to show that the program doesn't work. He left a note in a George Orwell book he borrowed from Boston Athenaeum Library. In case something happens to me, the note is in my inside jacket pocket. Just be very careful with Innes Tannah. She has me under observation and is covering up all of the evidence pointing to the program. She even has people in the agency." He hesitated, wondering if Jack was also an informant, then dismissed the idea and continued, "I trust you know what to do with this information."

Glenn hung up just as he arrived at the parking lot near the Black Falcon Cruise Terminal, once a busy destination for the now-discontinued Boston, Massachusetts, to Halifax, Nova Scotia, ferry. He parked in the corner of an empty lot looking out on to the Reserved Channel. He switched to the passenger side, moved a few items into the back seat, then reclined his seat back o provide a small, but comfortable sleeping area. He covered himself with a thermal blanket, slipped off his shoes, sipped some coffee, and tried to settle down for a nap. In the distance, a few cars zoomed down Summer Street, their passing headlights twinkling like stars. This view was putting him to sleep. Just as his head stopped bobbing, a loud noise came from nearby Drydock Avenue. His mind was at the cusp of sleep as a large, angry vehicle came closer and closer, its bright lights waking Glenn from his slumber.

* * *

Crash! The dining room table violently flew into the air and shattered on a back wall. Anne was glued to the back of the staircase wall, watching the scene from the side.

"I can hear you, Anne. I know you're on the staircase." Genne's voice was quiet, but clearly enraged and unstable.

She chose not to answer. She remained frozen on the staircase in case he was bluffing.

Genne continued his monologue. "It is only fair you have come to witness the destruction of one era and the birth of a new one." He threw a chair. It, too, shattered on the back wall, splinters flying in all directions, including one right beside Anne's face.

Anne covered her face, forcing her scream to remain inside for fear of being discovered.

Genne said, "I know they are coming. They know we are here. They know something is wrong." He punched a hole through the kitchen wall, then ripped half of it off with a single strong pull.

Anne was terrified he would soon choose her as his next target.

"Can't you see?" he proclaimed. "I must destroy the past to embrace the future!" He moved into the kitchen.

Anne quickly peeked into the living room, then withdrew in horror. The entire room was destroyed. Every piece of furniture was broken. Walls were scarred and ripped. The front door was barricaded with wreckage.

Genne opened the kitchen cupboard and began taking out dishes and cups then, with great satisfaction, he threw them into the living room wall, breaking them into thousands of pieces.

Anne shrieked at these sounds, knowing he picked her perfect kitchen on purpose to force her out of hiding.

He threw one plate really hard into the wall opposite where Anne was hiding. The force caused it to lodge in the wall. He threw another closer to the stairs and asked, "Why are you hiding from me, Anne?"

She heard him open another cupboard and took a chance, quickly sneaking across to the main hallway, inching toward the back exit, her only way out. The floor squeaked at her next step. She froze, then quickly backtracked.

Genne threw more cups and dishes, tracing her movement. He knew exactly where she was. "Where are you going, Anne?" he mocked in a singsong voice. He threw a frying pan into the closet door in the hallway. Again, the force of the throw pierced the wood and the pan stuck in the door.

Anne heard Genne approaching, coming closer and closer. He leaned on the other side of the wall and shouted, enraged, "I don't need you, Anne!"

This cry sent shivers down her body. She lost her footing and slipped down on the floor just as Genne's fist erupted through the wall above her then pulled back, ripping part of the wall away.

Anne was lying on the floor, terrified and speechless. Through the hole she caught sight of Genne's eyes, each a different color but both filled with madness. She gasped at seeing the rest of his face, cut up and bleeding badly.

* * *

Glenn slipped out of the vehicle just before a massive black truck smashed into his car, literally destroying it and launching it into the channel ahead. He rolled himself into the nearby port structure. He hid behind the main pillar, shoeless and without his gun. His thermal blanket was on the ground a few meters from the now detached and bent passenger door.

The truck's brakes screeched. Out stepped a slender figure, dressed in all black, including a mask with a single red Japanese symbol on it. The attacker moved quickly toward him.

Glenn launched himself toward his decapitated car door. He used it to shield himself just in time, as three precisely spread-out bullets penetrated it. One of them hit his forearm and went right through. He strained to contain the pain and keep the door up. He began moving toward the channel, but his pursuer would not allow that. At the first slip, the attacker shot Glenn in his foot. He fell, dropping his clumsy shield and revealing himself.

The attacker approached, holstering the pistol and unsheathing a long Japanese sword. She approached Glenn swiftly and placed the edge of the weapon directly beside his throat. Finally, the assassin spoke through some kind of electronic device in the mask, disguising their true identity, "Give me the file!"

Glenn was frozen on the ground, praying for his life. He slowly answered the request, "The file is in the car." Then he completely changed the tone of the scene and laughed. He continued with enjoyment, "No need for the mask, Innes. I know it's you." He strained to grin, pointing at the car slowly sinking in the channel. "Isn't it ironic that your very action made what you most seek ridiculously inaccessible." He continued to laugh. "I'm sure it will take you quite a bit of time to find it in the car." He then changed his tone, "And I've already alerted the police. I'm sure they will be here quite soon."

The attacker sheathed the sword, then moved closer. Glenn screamed in horror as the masked person grabbed his shot-up arm, stretched it, then pulled it hard to dislocate it. Tears poured down Glenn's face as the attacker said with quiet satisfaction, "I will break every bone in your body until you tell me exactly where the file is." The masked person stretched the bleeding arm again, arching it, then punched the elbow, shattering it. Glenn almost fainted from the pain. The assassin continued to his shot-up leg, again stretching it, dislocating it, and positioning for a devastating blow. Glenn muttered, half conscious, "In the trunk..." This time the attacker shattered both the tibia and fibula. Both were protruding through the skin. Glenn was fading, but he strained to whisper, "Inside the fabric lining." He managed to push out another phrase. "Please, stop..."

* * *

Anne was horrified at seeing Genne's face. She began crawling toward the stairs, but stopped at the edge, seeing the automatic vacuum still in one piece, hiding in the corner behind the trashed bookcase. Glenn heard her and moved in pursuit. Anne turned on the vacuum and dashed in the opposite direction, now back on her feet and adrenaline pumping through her veins.

Genne leaned in to find Anne, but instead found the vacuum getting ready to meet its ultimate challenge, cleaning up the devastation left in the living room. He turned back, hearing her move toward the exit.

Anne made it to the opposite side of the kitchen and glanced back to confirm Genne's distance. She froze, seeing Genne holding her precious vase. He spoke confidently, "You are not going anywhere, Anne."

She gathered all of the courage she could muster. "Genne, you are not well." She forced a compassionate tone to her voice. "Hon, you need help right now. Look what you did to your own face."

Genne smiled viciously. "There is nothing wrong with my face, Anne." Madness filled his eyes. "You are the last thing I have to let go."

"Then just let me go, Genne. You stay here. I'm sure JHJ will be here soon to take care of you."

Genne paused, fighting conflicting feelings, then insisted, "You and this stupid vase are my final sacrifices!"

Anne stood her ground. "You listen to me. I've been your wife for many years, putting up with your crap and tending to your insecurities. You will put that vase down and sit here till they come for you!"

Genne's eyes lifted, filled with madness. "No." He lifted the vase, ready to throw it.

Anne was frozen, faced with a choice to save herself or undertake the daring and deadly task of defending her family heirloom.

* * *

Glenn's pain rushed adrenaline into his body. He grabbed the leg of the assassin and pulled hard at the fabric, ripping it. The attacker pulled away, surprised at the desperate action. Glenn continued his assault. "Tell me, Innes, what happened between you and Lenny? Did you two get too close?"

The attacker stared at the broken, bleeding man spitting insults, trying to decide what to do next.

Glenn continued, "Did Lenny tell you that this new freedom is short-lived? That in time your old self will show its ugly face?"

The attacker grabbed Glenn's other arm and twisted it, commanding, "Stop!"

Glenn knew his end was near and responded, "No matter how much you want to remove the tattoos of your victims' sins, those scars will always remain."

Another crack and his scream filled the air as sirens sounded in the distance.

Glenn struggled to remain conscious amidst the pain. He forced another sentence through the blood in his mouth. "Innes, the very actions you are committing right now are demonstrating who you really are. You have betrayed Mannix. And you have betrayed yourself."

The attacker took off her mask and shouted, revealing her true voice. "No! It is you who forced my hand!" She approached again, angry, "You should have listened to my warnings!"

Glenn flopped onto his back, facing his opponent and choking on his blood. He struggled to say, "You can never run away from your past. You can only embrace it and learn from it and use it to create a better future version of yourself." Finally, his strength faded.

* * *

Genne screamed, ready to throw the vase at Anne. "I'm done with you!" In the background, he heard noises outside of the house. No doubt Mannix's security forces coming to contain him.

Anne stood her ground, now filled with conviction. She grabbed a kitchen knife from the chopping block on the counter and replied, "Not without a fight, you narcissistic, mega-ego, super idiot!"

Genne wasn't expecting that reaction, but nonetheless welcomed it. He threw the vase in Anne's direction. She ducked as it hit the screen door, then fell and broke into a few pieces.

Anne looked back, livid and energized. "Oh, no, you didn't!" She ripped the frying pan lodged from the closet door and rushed toward Genne. "I'm done taking care of your sorry ass! You … are … fired!"

Genne was getting ready to crush her skull with a single punch when the automated vacuum ran into his leg, distracting him just enough. In that same moment, a heavy iron pan painfully collided with his forehead with a force he never expected from his soon to be ex-wife. He momentarily lost his footing and reached out to support his body. Just then, a knife ran through his hand and into the kitchen cabinet he was holding. He screamed in unexpected pain as several finger tendons were cut. Just then, another well-placed blow from the frying pan knocked him down to the ground.

Anne was standing over him, full of adrenaline. "Now get your sorry, stupid, beat-up ass and get out of my house!" From behind her, she heard armed men enter the home.

As the security team entered the kitchen and surrounded them, she said, "You misguided idiot, your past doesn't hold you back. It's the foundation of a better future. I learned to love and embrace my past and who I am." She felt sorry for Genne. "I am beautiful with all of my strengths and weaknesses. I am unique and priceless." She pointed behind her. "You may break me like this family heirloom, but I will always get back on my feet." She dropped the pan on the ground. "I will always survive and move forward."

Private soldiers with H+ badges secured Glenn as JHJ walked in, shocked and horrified at the scene.

Anne removed her monitoring device and turned to JHJ. "I do not live in the fear of repeating yesterday's mistakes. I live in the conviction that I can shape a better tomorrow. There are no genes that can make you do this. It's a choice I learned to make!"

* * *

Glenn's words sounded deep inside of Innes, as if warming an icy stone hidden in her heart. She grabbed his neck and pulled something from her jacket. She stabbed his neck with something, and he woke up for a moment, mumbling a simple question, "Who are you?" She waited for a moment, then pulled out the small device now containing a sample of Glenn's blood. She placed his head down slowly and carefully while answering, "I don't really know anymore..." She was scared and surprised by her own answer. She stood, looked in the direction of the approaching emergency vehicles, then ran and jumped into the water, no doubt in search of the sinking car and her secret file.

The police approached first, and an ambulance followed. Emergency workers rushed to Glenn's body, examined him, then sprayed medical coagulation foam to stop his bleeding. They placed Glenn's body on a stretcher and rushed him to the nearby hospital.

Another FBI agent reached the scene and began asking questions, recognizing the victim. One of the emergency staff hurried to respond, "You must be Jack. Dispatch said you would be coming." The agent nodded.

The ER physician summarized the situation. "Your friend is very lucky. He obviously suffered many serious injuries, but none are life threatening." The physician paused, then reflected, "He either got lucky today or his assailant spared his life on purpose."

Chapter 27: The End and the Beginning

The talk show host re-read her notes as Mannix sat down across from her. A small white coffee table separated them, and two plain glasses filled with water dressed the sleek piece of furniture. Mobile cameras silently hovered around them. Boom and camera operators signaled their readiness, and the gaffer and grip did the same. The director gestured, and the host began to talk in a funny, intelligent, but geeky, British accent.

"Hello, my name is Jenny Nova and this is the Nexus. We reveal the biggest and hottest science stories." The host paused, turning toward Mannix, then continued as the camera panned out. "And today we have with us the world's most controversial genetic genius, Mannix Haldanne." Mannix waved to the camera as the host continued, "Tell me Dr. Haldanne—"

"Just Mannix, please," he interrupted.

Jenny obliged, "Of course." She gestured politely, then continued, "Mannix, what possessed you to forgo billions of dollars in profit and release your melanoma cure research to the world?"

Mannix smiled and answered humbly, "Jenny, this type of information does not belong in the greedy hands of corporations or politicians. In the true nature of science, it is meant to be shared freely for the betterment of the human race."

Jenny added, "It's not like you need more money anyway."

Mannix answered charmingly, "That's true as well. But even if I didn't, my father battled cancer for many years. This is my tribute to his life."

Jenny probed further as the camera zoomed in on his guest's face. "Why don't you tell us about your father? We know very little about him."

Mannix pulled back, but keeping a smile "Let's keep it that way." He took a sip of water, then continued awkwardly. "I am, as you already know, a very private creature. I keep my personal life very personal."

She responded, easing the tension. "Alright. Memo to myself. Do not cross examine the guest about his family, his personal hobbies, or about his crazy aunt Lydia."

Mannix laughed, relieved yet confused. "I don't have an Aunt Lydia? At least not that I know…"

Jenny waved comically. "We shall never speak her name. So, what now? We have the cure, but we don't know how to implement it."

Mannix's smile widened. "I may be able to help with that as well."

The host grinned. "I was expecting that."

Mannix continued, "In fact, if you don't mind, I would love to announce another breakthrough during this show."

Jenny began jumping and waving excitedly, "Are you bloody kidding me?!? An exclusive first-time reveal at my show? Why didn't you tell me earlier?" She exchanged looks with Mannix, slightly confused, then sat down and continued. "Sorry, mate, you did. You did tell me earlier. I totally forgot. Sorry." She then addressed the audience, "But you will all have to wait till the end of this show. You got it?"

Now she pivoted to Mannix again. "Okay, I have to ask you first. How did you manage in one year to accomplish what literally millions of scientists have tried to do for approximately a century?" She then added, joking, "You have a magic genie there or something?"

Mannix smiled slightly, then focused to indicate he was communicating something profound. "Jenny, all jokes aside for one moment if you don't mind." Jenny's eyes widened, but she remained quiet. Mannix continued "All I did was evolve our scientific method and looked at findings in a completely unbiased fashion."

Jenny's eyes remained wide while she asked calmly, but directly, "Are you saying our scientific research to date has been biased? You realize that by saying these words you face criticism and condemnation from the entire scientific community?"

Mannix explained eloquently, "I am, at my very heart, a scientist. It gives me no pleasure to state that our scientific methods are flawed. The very principles of our research create a partiality and even self-fulfilling prophecy, something we often refer to as observer bias. I was able to accomplish my research simply by removing this bias."

Jenny's stated at her guest. "Do continue…"

Mannix stood up, motioning with his hands. "As scientists, we observe the universe around us to develop theories. This is our first mistake. Our theories and understanding of them are completely biased products of our morality, our imperfect understanding, our emotional attachments, our pride, and our selfish dreams. We then formulate hypotheses and devise experiments to prove or disprove them. Then we tell ourselves we can remain impartial while evaluating the results of these experiments." He stopped and looked into the camera. "We are every bit as dogmatic and passionate as the religious zealots we ostracize and ridicule. And by placing ourselves in the center of the experiments, we make ourselves the very gods we reject and despise."

"Them are fightin' words, Mannix!" Jenny said.

Mannix was almost mesmerizing. "They are, but we need to be honest with ourselves and evolve. We need to admit our faults and grow above them."

The host questioned, "Spit it out, Mannix. What did you do to achieve your genetic research breakthroughs?"

Mannix gazed into the camera. "I used an idea that computer programmers and big-data scientists use in non-parametric algorithms. I removed the biased scientist, the partial hypothesis, and simply ran the experiment with no rules to contain its results. I used a supercomputer to index billions of genetic data samples to find its patterns."

"But the amount of data would be staggering. It would take years, if not centuries," Jenny interrupted.

Mannix responded, "Not true. We combined new quantum computing technologies and a self-adaptive algorithm. We received findings as early as six months into research, then continued receiving them incrementally since then for more than twelve months now."

"Wait! So this thing is still sequencing DNA as we speak?" Jenny interrupted again.

Mannix grinned with satisfaction. "That is correct. But more importantly it's showing us pure patterns based on hard data, not our biased hypotheses."

Jenny grinned back. "Two questions: Where is this magical research taking place and when can I visit it?"

Mannix replied, "My private facility in a highly secure location." Then added, "And probably never."

The host grimaced. "Why not?"

Mannix answered emphatically, "Because you would tell everyone!"

Jenny admitted, laughing, "That's true. I can't keep a secret." Then she said, "And for that very reason we shall not hesitate any longer!" She motioned for Mannix to sit back down, then said, "Okay, so what's the big announcement?"

Mannix delayed, increasing the tension in the audience.

The host was getting impatient. "Come on, don't make us wait right after you insult our very honor."

Mannix savored the reveal, "This research shows far more than how to cure cancer." He waited for people to hang on his words, "It also reveals how we can evolve."

Jenny was blown away. "Whaaat? … Aunt Lydia?"

Mannix continued, "Imagine combining the best DNA sequences all together to make us stronger, smarter, more resilient, sexier, healthier, and perhaps even overcoming death itself."

"Making a superhuman?" she offered

Mannix shook his head. "Not making. Rather, us becoming. A process through which an average person like you and me can become far more than they could ever imagine."

Jenny intentionally let her jaw drop, then used her hand to push it back up.

Mannix ignored her shenanigans. "This is not just a theory. I am here to announce this is now a reality."

Jenny repeated the jaw act again, this time toward the camera.

Mannix continued, "Today I will reveal proof of a procedure that took place approximately one month ago. We took an average citizen and altered his genetic makeup to achieve superior DNA. This resulted in literally thousands of ground-breaking physical and mental improvements. These results will speak for themselves."

Jenny raised hers hand comically, as if in a class waiting her turn to speak.

Mannix gestured to the host, appearing confused. "Yes, Jenny?"

She swallowed, then spoke slowly, as if not believing the words coming out of her mouth. "You altered the genetic makeup of a live human subject?" She was beside herself. "But how? In what country? Was that procedure even legal?"

Mannix became slightly defensive. "I assure you, the procedure was completely legal and with the patient's full consent."

"So who is it and can we talk to him about the procedure?"

"Absolutely. His name is Genne Manning. The science community and media alike will have full access to him, including various post-procedure assessments." Then he stood again, gazed into the camera, and drove the message home. "This person is the first real proof, proof that we are ready to evolve as a species. We are ready to be reborn into something much greater. We are capable of so much more than we can even imagine. We can overcome our physical limitations, our weaknesses, and our faults that hold us back. We can create a new world free of disease, grief, and even death."

He managed one last sentence before the announcement ended. "Join me on this ultimate journey…"

Book 2 Teasers

Some of these chapters will appear in the next book.

A. Extraction

Mannix boarded his private plane while Innes and the others sedated and secured various patients, including Genne.

He was alone in his private bathroom. With nobody around, he allowed his feelings to surface. He was extremely frustrated and disappointed about Genne failing to integrate back into society. This success story was so critical to the larger plan he was going to execute in the next twelve months. This setback would cost him time he simply didn't have.

Mannix screamed and punched the metal wall, which were thick and soundproof. He knew nobody would bother him. This violent expression reminded him to contain his emotion. He turned on the faucet and ran some cold water. He filled his hands, then submerged his face, sending shivers down his back. He released his hands, letting the water spill into the sink and breathed in slowly.

He pressed on the top-right corner of the mirror. It flashed quickly with a dim green blink, confirming his DNA scan. To the right, a small compartment emerged from the wall. Inside were two small metal containers and a small glass bottle full of pills. He first reached out and extracted one shiny blue capsule from the bottle. He placed it under his tongue and waited till it dissolved. He then opened the other two containers. They were filled with liquid. He carefully reached to his eyes and one by one removed his contact lenses. He looked back at himself in the mirror, his face still dripping with cold water. His eyes were not just different colors. Both irises were filled with multiple colors. Not just two or three. Rather, there was a rainbow of twenty to thirty colors in each eye. He closed them and took another deep breath, slowing his mind and purging the thoughts that overwhelmed him.

His meditation was interrupted by a short ping on a wall com device. "Mannix, we are ready and cleared to depart."

He surfaced from his daze to answer succinctly, "Proceed."

Mannix dried his face, exited the bathroom, and entered a small personal room. He sat down in a large armchair and strapped himself in with a seatbelt.

At the same time, Innes walked in with a bottle of water and two glasses. She placed these items securely on a small table in front of them, then sat across and secured her seatbelt as well. She was silent for a few moments till Mannix started the conversation. "Is Genne secure?"

Innes confirmed in Japanese, "Hai hai, sensei"

Mannix connected with her evading eyes. "I know what happened with Agent Abbot. We'll talk about that later." He paused, taking a controlled breath. "For now, we're focusing on the recovery of our greatest asset, Genne."

"JHJ has already developed a program that we will execute as soon as we reach the facility."

Mannix drank some of the water. "It's not that easy. Unlike our other patients, he is a U.S. citizen. We cannot cage him or contain him for long."

"Perhaps we should keep him sedated a little longer?" Innes suggested.

Mannix pondered this possibility, then answered, "No. We don't have time. Keep him in a secure area away from the others. Fix his facial scarring and ensure he contacts his family so his absence is not reported. We don't want the U.S. Navy invading our facility in the Atlantic Ocean. Remember, Genne is our proof that this DNA modification works."

"Perhaps we could reprogram him," Innes suggested as an alternative.

"Only if absolutely necessary," Mannix insisted, taking another sip of water as the craft accelerated rapidly, tilted, then began rising sharply.

Innes confirmed, again in Japanese, "Hai hai, sensei"

Mannix looked at his glass, which was almost empty, then remembered, "I assume you were successful in acquiring Agent Abbot's blood sample?"

Her eyes lowered with guilt and shame. "Hai." After a moment of silence, she built the courage to ask, "May I ask for what purpose we acquired this?"

Mannix savored his answer. "Let's just say I have certain plans for Agent Abbot..."

B. Geneva

Mannix was looking out of a large window at The Palais Des Nations in Geneva. He was waiting just outside the Council Chamber in Section C of the vast building, admiring a unique sculpture located in a slightly wooded area in front of the building. It was the largest and arguably the strangest sculpture created by Michelangelo Pistoletto, a late Italian artist. Made of almost 200 large stones, each approximately half a meter cubed. Together, it was forty-two meters long and twenty meters wide, and was made up of three circles. He knew the name of the sculpture, *Rebirth*. Its meaning was well rooted in the reconfigured infinity sign, typically consisting of two circles, but here altered to include a third one signifying a rebirth of humanity, of society, a new world.

Not too far from it stood another sculpture, a large Armillary sphere. This unique celestial model had earth at the center of the universe, the sun and other planets rotating around it. However, instead of planets it incorporated zodiac, Chinese, Greek, and Latin zodiac symbols. This four-meter art piece weighed close to six thousand kilograms. Although functional and rotating during its official inauguration in 1939, it had been stagnant since 1942. The motor not in use since 1945. Mannix thought it was ironic that the only time the sphere did work was during the height of the Nazi regime in Europe. He reflected on the meaning of these two sculptures. One a reminder of the infinity of human potential, the other a reminder of human arrogance and antiquated thought based on pure dogma once opposing science.

An attendant approached and interrupted him, "Dr. Haldanne, I presume." He was a clean-shaven man in his thirties, formally dressed in a black suit with a white shirt, a bowtie, and a nametag bearing the UN insignia.

Mannix met his eyes confidently and answered, "You presume correctly."

The attendant responded, "Very well, sir. The United Nations and World Health Organization are waiting for you in the Council Chamber. They are eager to hear your proposal on solving the world's population and hunger problems." He pointed his entire arm sharply in the direction of a large two-door entrance, then led him in, saying "Right this way…"

C. Cairo in Darkness

Innes sat on a small, tight patio in a suburban Cairo coffeehouse. Egyptian coffee was dark and strong but felt very familiar. Her mother used to make it late at night. The smell brought back many warm memories. She scanned the Café. Worn-out wooden and wicker chairs were full of squeaky character. Tables were small, primarily made of brass and glass. The streets were busy at this late hour. Large antique mirrors hang on the walls, making the place seem much larger. Tiny tin ceiling lamps illuminated the table while allowing visitors to keep a level of dark anonymity. A few older men enjoyed their shisha tobacco from hookah pipes.

A slim, middle-aged man dressed in a black short-sleeved shirt approached her slowly. His company, two beefier men, held back about thirty feet away. He approached with his hands in front and greeted Innes, "As-Salaam-Alaikum".

Innes recognized the man from the distance. She replied courteously, "Wa-Alaikum-Salaam. It is good to see you, Mo. It has been far too long." She stood up to half-embrace him.

The man gave a reassuring look to his backup and sat down across the table. He asked immediately, "What brings you to Cairo, the city that never sleeps?"

She took another sip of coffee and stated, "I have something to offer you ... Something to help your cause..."

The man responded cautiously. "I see ... And what do you seek in return?"

Innes responded confidently, "A safe place by your side, my dear cousin. I will aid you in your life quest to establish a true caliphate in Egypt. You know I can be ... very resourceful."

Mo continued his questioning, "Safe place ... from whom?"

They were interrupted by a young waiter. Mo quickly ordered some coffee and dismissed him.

Innes replied, "My previous employers ..."

Mo smiled, then explained, "Dear Innes, your recent life is just as interesting as your youthful rebellion and your unfortunate past with Yakuza. I'm afraid I cannot help you. My organization already faces many enemies. We are not interested in acquiring any new ones. That would result in an unfortunate distraction from what we're trying to accomplish."

Innes leaned forward. Her face became visible. Mo was slightly startled by her eyes in two different colors. She didn't back down. "You're not seeing the big picture, Mo. I have something far more valuable to offer than my shady past." She leaned down, opened her purse, and removed a tiny metal box. She opened it to show a military-grade encased data card "This will surely turn the tide in your favor. Your brotherhood no longer has to fear those who oppose you. This weapon is like nothing you have seen before."

Mo quickly slid the case into his jacket pocket then asked cautiously, "What is this? A weapon? Are you going to start a war? This is not the place to discuss these matters."

The waiter interrupted them again, bringing Mo a cup of dark coffee. He also checked with Innes if she needed more. She waved him off and he walked to another table.

Innes led on, "This is not another dirty bomb you use to kill politicians or tourists like your brotherhood did at Luxor, Sainai, Dahab, and other places. This weapon will wipe out all the Israeli … everywhere."

Mo was visibly shocked. "But how? That would be a global genocide!"

Innes pushed on confidently. "It's a genetically engineered virus targeting DNA sequences unique to a specific group of people. Have your men check the data. When you're ready, provide an extraction location for me and the weapon." She paused to expand on her last statement. "I think this gift is worth far more than what I ask in return."

Mo shook his head, still in disbelief, "And so it will be. Give me a day or two to review this information."

Innes stood. "Very well. You know how to find me." She placed her hand on his shoulder affectionately, then walked off.

Mo finished his coffee, pulled out some cash to pay, then began walking to his Mercedes, now joined by his two bodyguards. In his mind, two words repeated over and over. *Genetic Genocide.* He wasn't sure if such an act would be interpreted by his brotherhood as a holy weapon or sheer madness.

D. The Motley Crew

A well-dressed gentleman entered the boardroom filled with an eclectic collection of military and civilian experts. He spoke immediately. "Welcome. My code name is Edward. I'm from Interpol, and I'll be spearheading this covert operation. Why don't we all introduce ourselves."

He pointed to his left, where a woman in her forties started awkwardly. "Hi. My name is … my codename is Russo." She was embarrassed about stumbling, then regained her confidence. "I've spent several days in Mannix's facility. My husband underwent the procedure there a few months ago." She paused, unsure what else to say. Edward wrapped up "Russo will provide us with valuable insights about the location, security forces, operational protocols, and key staff involved."

Edward pointed to the next person, an unshaven man in a wheelchair with numerous bruises and scars. The man introduced himself as codename Abbot. I'm from the FBI. I know we don't typically get involved in affairs outside the U.S. borders, but I'm an exception. I have extensive knowledge of Mannix's Genetic Prisoner Reform Program that is taking place in the facility.

The next person jumped in. "My codename is Hothead. I lead a small team of Navy Seals specializing in zero-casualty extractions. We are few, but we are the best. We know this mission is very risky. That's how we like it." He took a sip of his drink, then placed his glass on the table confidently.

Edward pointed to a classy woman in business dress. She spoke with a French accent. "My codename is Charlie. I'm a senior agent at the French DPSD. I specialize in counterespionage as well as self-guided micro-explosives. It's a sexier, more elegant way of blowing things into thousands of tiny pieces." She smiled and gently pointed to the next person.

The next person was a sharp geek wearing a HUD device on his head. "My codename is Monty. MI6 sent me here to assist with this mission. I'm an expert in bioengineering and human genetics, as well as quantum computing. And don't get me started on my IQ." Edward let everyone know immediately. "Be careful with Monty. He has a sharp, narcissistic wit."

Ed moved to the next person, who stood quietly. "Last, but not least, we have the captain of this unique vessel. We just call him Captain. While he is a man of very few words, he is also a great chef." The grumpy man's face barely moved.

Edward took off his leather gloves and pressed his hand on to the table. The table scanned his imprint and DNA, then began to project three-dimensional tactical information as he continued, "Here are our orders. First, gather intelligence on Mannix's secret and heavily guarded facility. Second, infiltrate and sabotage the facility with minimum casualties. We don't know who is currently undergoing treatments there. Likely, the world's richest and most influential individuals. Third, extract Mannix and deliver him to Interpol for interrogation and incarceration. During this mission, we have unlimited access to Interpol's surveillance resources, espionage equipment, satellite weaponry, and so on. Any questions?"

Charlie raised her hand and asked, "Why the secrecy? Why not simply attack and take over his facility?"

Edward smiled, expecting the question. "Three reasons, dear Charlie. First, Mannix has numerous government contracts protecting him. Actions you just described would put all of these at risk, not to mention being a global PR nightmare. Second, remember these waters are no longer international property. He owns them. Essentially, an invasion would be deemed an act of war. That's the last thing we want. Third, shared agency intelligence agrees that a covert mission is the only way to safely extract Mannix. He is too heavily guarded and monitored."

Edward continued, "To be honest, our intelligence about this facility is extremely limited. Interpol estimates less than a seven percent chance of mission success."

Abbott grimaced and contributed, "Perhaps we can improve our odds ..."

Edward asked curiously, "What did you have in mind?"

Abbott approached the table and pressed a few buttons. A photo appeared as he answered, "Let's get Innes Tannah on our side..."

Behind the story…

Visit the website to continue your journey into this exciting world. Uncover new details about these characters. Delve into the rich historical, philosophical, and scientific backdrop of the story. Most importantly, engage with the writer to help shape future books.

www.metamorphosisbookseries.com

Acknowledgements

Cover image provided by Gordon Johnson

https://pixabay.com/users/gdj-1086657/

https://pixabay.com/vectors/dna-deoxyribonucleic-acid-people-2789567/